BETWEEN

DANIEL FROST

COVER ART BY FRANK BERGER

ARCTIC WOLF PUBLISHING

This book is dedicated to my wife and daughter and for their never ending faith and patience with me.

PREFACE

The Shadow King was annoyed.

Lightning flashed across the sky illuminating the room, but there wasn't much to see, only some moldy furniture, a few threadbare rugs, some crumbling paintings of long-lost wars, a few rusted suits of armor, and torches that didn't need to burn—the Shadow King had no need for these things. There were padlocks on iron doors, and black ivy that grew up the walls and around the ceiling, twisting its way all through the throne that he was currently occupying.

If you happened to be unlucky enough to be in that room with the Shadow King, you would notice that the darkness radiated from him, and he was really nothing more than smoke and shadow and malevolence.

Knock, knock.

The Shadow King lifted his head and the locks fell from the door, and an unlucky guard poked his head into the room.

"Master, we've found the boy."

The shadowy apparition rose up and up from the throne and drifted across the room until his crowned head was only inches from the unlucky guard's grey-green face. The apparition solidified ever so slightly and brought his fiery gaze down on the guard, waiting for the slightest reason to snuff out this messenger's existence, but the guard stayed silent.

Like a mighty python the Shadow King coiled around his chest compressing his ribs in an iron grip attempting to wrench free any lies that might be hiding under the surface. The guard quaked in his muddy boots, but said nothing more.

Satisfied, the hard edges of the Shadow King relaxed slightly and he released his grip, recoiling back across the room and melted into the shadows. "Excellent, where is he now?"

With a gasp, the guard eased back a few paces. "We've locked him in the dungeon, Sire."

There was silence and a cold chill ran down the guard's spine and panic began tightening its grip on him once more. The darkness swirled and an unreadable face nearly as large as the room materialized from the shadows in front of him. The guard started to tremble, but then the features of the shadow softened and a thin crack slowly spread across the face and ever so slightly curled upwards.

"Wonderful, just wonderful… now throw away the key."

The guard stumbled backwards from the room and slammed the door shut behind him.

…

Hardly perceptible within the blackness of the room the smile grew just bit wider.

CHAPTER ONE

Crinkly Yellow Pages

Chance found the crinkled yellow pages on top of the bookshelf. Actually she found a big yellow and orange striped tabby cat with lovely blue eyes up there and the pages just happened to fall down when she grabbed for the cat.

She was in an old bookshop that had a front door with a little bell attached to it that tinkled every time it was opened. It had dusty old books stacked in nice neat rows on dark wooden shelves that disappeared into the shadows as they ran to the back wall. The regulars of the shop were dusty as well, and maybe just a bit stale, with names like Gertrude and Matilda and Edward.

Miss Plink owned the shop and lived in the rooms upstairs with her fat, round cats that had pushed-in faces and bushy tails. Chance thought that Miss Plink was probably as old as the shop, and that she smelled liked mothballs and old people, and had a caved-in face like her cats, with a chin that stuck out too far because her teeth had long since gone missing and she sometimes forgot to wear her dentures.

She didn't much like it when Chance played with her cats and let her know this every time she came in the shop. "Now, Chance," she would say, "you leave those cats be. They're my little babies, and they don't like to be picked up or played with… cats just don't like those things. They like quiet time, and milk with honey, and chasing mice… but they don't like little girls dragging them around and pulling their tails and batting their paws."

But Chance did none of these things. She scratched behind their ears and rubbed their bellies and stroked the soft fur on their backs and below their chins, and she was sure they liked it.

"But Miss Plink, I think the cats like me to pet them, and play with them."

Miss Plink wouldn't say a word, just look down her nose and tilt her spectacles forward while raising her thick grey eyebrows which crinkled up her forehead. So Chance would just sulk off to the back of the shop and play with the cats anyway, because she knew they liked it.

She spotted the big yellow and orange striped cat sitting on top of the shelf watching her with detached interest in a way only a cat can.

"Come here, Shere Khan, I'll rub your belly," said Chance, remembering his name from the last time Miss Plink had gone looking for him.

The top of the bookshelf was too high for her to reach, so she dragged over a sturdy chair and pushed it up against the books, watching to make sure no one was looking. When the coast was clear she pulled herself up and stretched for the cat, lifting up on her tiptoes to reach a bit farther.

"Come on, cat." She extended her fingers as far as she could reach, but with no luck.

Chance got down, pulled a particularly plump old book from the shelf, laid it down flat on the chair, and then climbed back up, stepping on the book to get a bit higher. This time she was able to reach the cat, but accidentally yanked his tail, cringing when she thought of the scolding Miss Plink was about to give her. The cat yowled and leaped off the shelf, which made everyone turn and look at the little girl in red top boots, and faded jeans, and a shabby grey T-shirt doing exactly what she wasn't supposed to do.

Miss Plink snorted, and made her way to Chance, who was still standing on the stool. "Miss Counter, I believe I mentioned that you were specifically not to torment my cats."

Chance sighed and knew this wasn't the

time to argue. "I'm sorry, Miss Plink."

She stepped down from the stool, gently picked up the book she'd been standing on, and wiped clean the footprints with her shirt. With an innocent smile she placed the book back on the shelf and gave it a soft little pat.

Miss Plink moved the stool back to where it belonged. She pulled a neat little hanky from one of the many pockets on her vest and absentmindedly dusted the stool and the shelf, but the dust drifted back in place, which didn't seem to bother her in the least. When she turned her attention back to Chance, she saw the crinkly yellow pages lying on the floor, and wavered for just an instant. With a little groan, that didn't sound quite like a normal old person's groan, Miss Plink bent down and picked up the pages quickly sorting through them.

Chance was pretty sure that the yellowy pages, dried glue, and dusty cat prints should be enough evidence to prevent Miss Plink from thinking she had torn the pages from a book, but there was something about the look in Miss Plink's eyes that made her worry.

Chance crinkled up her nose and watched as Miss Plink shuffled through the pages. "Where do you think they came from?" asked the little girl.

"From the top of the shelf of course," said Miss Plink.

Chance peered up at the top of the shelf. "Hmm… the cat must have been sitting on them and pushed them off when he jumped away," she said, slightly relieved.

Miss Plink nodded, and set the pages down on one of the nearby desks and began to scrutinize them more carefully. She gently rubbed the paper between her fingers, and with a bemused look on her face she looked over at Chance. "Can't say I've ever seen this size or texture of paper before—very strange."

Miss Plink, with Chance in tow,

methodically marched around the little shop measuring the size of the pages against other books in the store, mumbling whenever she couldn't find a match.

"Doesn't look like they belong to any book here," said Chance.

Miss Plink didn't answer.

Chance took a quick peek at the pages when she stopped to check them against another row of books that they obviously couldn't have come from. "Looks like they may have come from a storybook or art book?"

Miss Plink still didn't answer.

"Since they don't belong to any book in the store, do you think I can have them—I quite fancy the look of them?" said Chance with an innocent look on her face.

Miss Plink stopped in her tracks and spun around on her heels to face the little girl. "Now why should I give you these pages, especially after the way you found them?"

"Well... I suppose because they don't seem to fit in any of the books here, so I guess you're probably just going to throw them away, and that would be an awful shame."

Miss Plink was about to fire back, but held her tongue when she saw that the girl was being sincere. Her crinkly old face, that probably hadn't smiled in years, softened ever so slightly and she pulled out a chair from a nearby desk and took a seat... gesturing to Chance to do the same.

CHAPTER TWO

Just By Chance

The little bell on the door tinkled and the hinges squeaked, but Miss Plink never took her eyes off Chance.

"You see, Chances," Miss Plink said, adding the 'es' to her name which only her mom did when she was in trouble. "This is a little town and everybody knows everybody's little secrets, and bookshops are great places to hear everything that's going on."

"Yes, ma'am, I mean, no ma'am. I didn't realize that," said Chance, wondering how this had anything to do with her and her little misdeed.

"Let me get to the point, Miss Counter, do you know how you came to get your name?"

Chance's leg tickled and she reached down and scratched her calf, realizing that the big yellow and orange striped tabby cat named Shere Khan had just rubbed up against her.

"Of course," said Chance.

"Your mother was on a commercial airline flight over the Pacific Ocean, flying home from a business trip, and your father was on a totally different flight hundreds of miles away returning to his home from a vacation on the west coast of Mexico. Your dad's flight was diverted north, then west over the Pacific to avoid *Barbara*, a raging hurricane with intense thunderstorms and winds that spawned tornadoes strong enough to wipe entire towns off the map. ...You know I never could figure out why they don't name those storms differently, I mean *Barbara* is just a ridiculous name for a deadly hurricane, but I digress."

"Yes, ma'am I know the story very well," said Chance politely. "I agree, as well, that *Barbara* is a silly name for a storm that wiped out half of Southern California."

"The aircraft your mother was on got diverted as well, flying south to avoid the storm. Unfortunately the massive hurricane changed direction and both aircraft, still hundreds of miles apart, got caught in the maelstrom. Both planes struck the ocean, and broke apart." Miss Plink paused for a moment, and held out her hanky. "Are you OK dear? If you need to cry I understand, this *is* a tragic story."

"No ma'am, I'll be fine," said Chance with the sincerest smile she could muster.

"Of course you are dear... stay strong." Miss Plink sighed. "It turns out both your mother and father *did* survive the crash, and miraculously escaped in life rafts."

Chance interrupted. "And somehow, against all odds, and even though the planes had crashed hundreds of miles apart... they both ended up on the same small, uninhabited island 42 miles north of the Fijian island Vanua Levu, or formerly known as Sandalwood Island," said

Chance, hoping Miss Plink might actually *understand* she knew something about this story."

Miss Plink just grinned back. "While on that island your parents fell in love, and soon after their rescue they were married, and you, young Chance N. Counter were born."

Shere Khan leapt up into Chance's lap and circled round and round, kneading his paws on her pants and waving his tail across her face until he was satisfied, then he curled up into a happy little purring ball of fluff and closed his eyes. Chance smiled and scratched behind the cat's ears until his purring began to distract Miss Plink.

Miss Plink watched the content cat doze off in the girl's lap and studied the young girl for a moment. "Do you understand why I told you this story Miss Counter?"

Chance looked up from the cat and realized Miss Plink might actually be getting to the end of the story. "Yes Miss Plink, you told me this story so I would know why I was given such an unusual name."

Miss Plink smiled. "Child, did you actually think that I'm so old I didn't realize you must already know your parents' history?"

"No Miss Plink, I mean yes Miss Plink... I mean I'm not really sure as I hear the story so often."

Then Miss Plink did the oddest thing and she pushed the crinkled yellow book pages with the interesting illustrations on them over to Chance. "I imagine you must."

Chance ran her hand over the pages and tried to smooth them out. "Thank you... these are very nice, but why are you giving them to me?"

Miss Plink smiled. "Do you know what a pachinko machine is?"

Chance squinted up her eyes and made like she was thinking. "Not really, I suppose I don't."

"A pachinko machine is mostly used for gambling and resembles a vertical pinball machine, but with no flippers and a number of relatively small balls. The player fires a single ball up into the machine, controlling only its initial speed. The ball then falls down through a dense forest of pins bouncing back and forth with no particular path to follow. The ball eventually lands at the bottom and most of the time is lost, but occasionally they drop into certain pockets and the player wins," said Miss Plink.

Chance frowned. "That doesn't sound like too much fun."

"No it really isn't unless you like to gamble; because that's all it is... just a gamble where you think the ball might land."

"I'm sorry Miss Plink, but I really don't understand why you're telling me this?" said Chance.

Miss Plink grinned. "The pachinko

machine is the definition of *random*; the balls just fall to the bottom with no definite aim or purpose. But Chance, life is more than that. Your life, my dear, nor your parents', has anything to do with *random*," said Miss Plink ignoring the tinkling little bell as more customers came in the store.

Chance shook her head. "That's just not how it feels sometimes. You should try spending some time in my muddy red boots. The strangest, most random things happen to me all the time and I never know what is going to happen next."

"I can understand why you must think like this, especially with your parents' history and all."

Chance smiled a lopsided smile and nodded.

"How about Rube Goldberg, have you ever heard of him or his inventions?" asked Miss Plink.

Chance shook her head still a bit

confused. "No I'm afraid I haven't."

"Rube Goldberg is best known for a series of popular cartoons he created depicting complex devices that perform simple tasks in indirect, convoluted ways—now known as Rube Goldberg machines. One of his famous creations was the *Self-Operating Napkin*," said Miss Plink as she took in a deep breath. "The 'Self-Operating Napkin' is activated when a soup spoon is raised to the operator's mouth, pulling on a string which is attached to both the spoon and a ladle, pulling the string thereby jerks the ladle, which throws a cracker past a parrot that's perched on the machine."

"A real parrot?" asked Chance.

"Yes a real parrot, now please let me continue."

"Sure, sorry."

"OK, the parrot jumps after cracker, and because his perch is balanced like a titer-totter, it tilts when he hops in the air, hence upsetting a small container of seeds that was used as the parrot's counter balance which now pours into a pail. The extra weight in pail pulls on a cord, which opens and lights an automatic cigar lighter, setting off a skyrocket which causes a knife to cut a string that is tied to a pendulum on a clock. The napkin is attached to the pendulum and can now swing back and forth, thereby wiping the operator's chin."*

"Wow that sounds so cool," said Chance as she screwed up her eyes. "And I don't mean to be disrespectful, but I still don't see how this has anything to do with the crinkly yellow pages that fell off the top of the shelf and why you're giving them to me."

The bell on the door tinkled again, but Miss Plink didn't even flinch. "You my dear, are an awfully smart girl. Do you really think all the crazy things that have been happening to you are

*Wolfe, Maynard Frank, "Rube Goldberg: Inventions!" Simon & Schuster, November 20, 2000

in a silly game, or do you really think your life is a bit more like a complex contraption with many seemingly insignificant moving parts that once all set in motion actually add up to something?"

Chance didn't know how to answer.

Miss Plink smiled and poked the book pages with her finger.... "Those, Chance, are for you."

Chance said nothing just stared at the crinkly yellow pages that fell off the top of an old book shelf, pushed off by a yellow and orange striped tabby cat with lovely blue eyes.

The cat purred a tad louder and looked up at the little girl as if he knew what she was thinking. Chance scratched behind his ears and he looked away curling back into a ball on her lap.

Miss Plink stood up from her chair and plucked the content cat from Chance's lap setting him on the floor and pushing him away. "Go on,

Shere Khan, get on upstairs and have some dinner." Miss Plink looked back at Chance. "And I think it's best for you to be getting home for some dinner yourself... I have customers to attend to."

Chance hesitated for a minute then got up and gently put the pages from the book into a tattered leather backpack she always carried with her, and slipped her arms through the straps. She said goodbye to Miss Plink and to Shere Khan, who hadn't moved an inch from the spot where Miss Plink set him down, and was half way out the door before she turned. "Miss Plink, thanks... thanks a lot."

Miss Plink dusted off the cover of an old book of fairy tales and handed it to a little boy who grabbed it and ran off to one of the couches. "Just let me know how it turns out... I'm always up for a good story."

The weather was dreary and a wet mist hung over the little town, giving it a fuzzy, hazy appearance. It had started to drizzle, but Chance was prepared with a Mickey Mouse umbrella. She slung open the umbrella and leapt off the curb into the first puddle she could find. Unlike the weather, her mood was good, her life may actually be more than it seems—a *complex contraption* she thought to herself, how exciting.

CHAPTER THREE

New Things to See

The day after they moved to town Chance went exploring. It wasn't really a small town or for that matter a big town, but her parents said it was the right size town for them. It had a town square, and a main street, and a few churches with spires. There were a few good restaurants in the town, but most of them served weird food, in little portions, with all kinds of green leafy things, and bad tasting sauces.

There were three elementary schools, three middle schools, and two high schools, which really made no sense unless all the middle school kids moved away before high school, but apparently no one seemed to notice but her. The town had a couple of interesting parks with gigantic old oak trees that had branches perfect for climbing, and huge knot holes that you could stick your head all the way into—which turns out isn't such a good idea.

By the end of the first week Chance had explored each of the parks making sure she had climbed every tree, and determined which one had the softest moss beneath it so when she fell out it wouldn't hurt so much. For her second week she spent some of her time looking for animals and snakes, and was excited when she spotted a fox chasing a snake, but the snake slithered down a hole and got away which turned out to be a bit disappointing. She also found a few ponds, but sadly, none of them had alligators or piranhas or anything else really dangerous, so she spent time skipping stones over the smooth water and counting how many skips she could make, eight incidentally, but she quickly became bored of that and moved on.

Once she was convinced she had explored the parks and the surrounding areas as well as she could and that no hidden treasure was overlooked she turned her attention to the town square and the little shops that lined the main street.

There she found an old drugstore that had fresh squeezed lemonade and oddly flavored drinks from an old-timey soda fountain. The drugstore kept her occupied for a couple of days while she had money in her pocket, but when that ran out she decided to investigate the other shops and went from store to store to see what they had to offer.

There were stores that carried dress clothing for ladies and suits for men, there were stores full of ugly uncomfortable furniture that no one honestly would want to sit in, and there were shops full of old dusty things you would find in your grandmother's attic, but none of these places really kept her interest for very long so she kept looking for more things to do.

By the end of the second week she found

herself sitting on the curb in front of the drugstore wishing she had a bit more money to buy a vanilla soda with a splash of lime when an old blue van with out of state plates smashed into a parking meter right in front of her. The meter crashed to the ground and all its change poured out, much of it tumbling onto her shoe. She wasn't a greedy little girl so she only picked up enough change to buy the drugstore out of gummy worms so that she could find out how many would fit in her mouth at one time, plus the vanilla soda with a splash of lime, but that didn't taste nearly as good as she thought it would.

While she contemplated which record book she should notify of this gastronomical feat her stomach began making odd noises and her gut started to cramp. Apparently sixteen gummy worms, one gummy shark (must have got stuck in the wrong candy pot), and a vanilla soda with a splash of lime could also make you properly sick, so she decided it was time to go home... quickly.

The buildings and shops were all connected in long rows and made the town like a maze and even though she lived less than a mile away as the crow flies, she had to walk a dozen blocks up the street just so she could go around the corner and walk halfway back to intersect the street she lived on. But her stomach was in no mood for this, and walking that far was out of the question so she improvised and looked for a shortcut that would get her home as fast as possible.

She found an alley that split between the buildings a couple of blocks up from the drugstore and knew that a dirty alley wasn't a good place for a little girl to pass through, but nevertheless she found herself doing this anyway. It was a dusty, smelly old alley, full of trash and moldy water. Her mother would never allow her to cut through a place like that, and frankly she knew she shouldn't, but it was an emergency and such rules didn't apply at times like that. About halfway down the alley she realized it dead ended into a bricked up wall with no door, and other than making a quick mental note not to bother with the place again she ran back out and found another alley that did cut all the way through, allowing her to get home just in time.

That was how she spent the first two weeks in the new town—exploring the parks and the shops and the soda fountain.

Chance lived with her mother and father in a three story townhouse—it had an attic at the very top and a basement at the very bottom; the basement was really a room built into the side of a hill that the real estate agent called a basement but really wasn't, and a kitchen and living room on the second floor and bedrooms on the top floor. Her room was the third room on the right when you came up the stairs; she chose it because it had a cool, winding staircase that led into the attic where she spent a lot of her time. That was where she was now, sitting at a little desk, studying the crinkled yellow pages that she had found in the bookshop.

The pictures were very good, so good they looked like photographs, but when she looked at them very closely she could see that they were actually painted on the pages. Each one was amazingly detailed, and by the feel of them she was sure that they were definitely painted there.

She didn't know how she knew it, but sure as the sun would come up the next morning she knew they were special, and though she was not some art expert she could tell they were painted by one of the Masters her mom raved about when they toured those museums—Leonardo da Vinci or Michelangelo or Raphael or any one of the other names her parents told her about. The strangest bit about them was that they were really old, or at least she thought they were because they were yellow and crinkly. It was the scenes on each one that made them strange… the places in the pictures shouldn't have existed when they were painted, but the detail was so perfect and the scene so timely that the artist could only have been standing at that spot to paint them. Those pages, she thought, were an anachronism, because those places could not have been around when those pictures were painted. Of course the artist could have been painting the future, but they looked so real it was hard to believe that they were just from someone's imagination.

There were four of them in all; one was a picture of a weather beaten barn surrounded by cornfields and a red tractor way in the background; another was a bedroom in a creepy house with cobwebs in the corners and furniture all covered in dusty blankets. The third picture she thought might be some kind of train station, or at least she thought it should be, because at one edge of the page she could see people lining up and milling about like people do when they are waiting for something, and at the other edge of the page she saw the big round headlight of an old-time train with a big white puffy cloud of steam billowing out from the exhaust stack; and the fourth picture she recognized.

She hadn't noticed it the first time she flipped through them, but each picture had one thing in common: each picture had a door painted in it. It really didn't look like any door you would normally see, made of wood or metal or glass, but more like a shadow that had a little doorknob and was slightly cracked open so light was showing around the edges.

Each picture had this little door painted there, and on each of the paintings it seemed out of place, hidden in the background, and somehow frightening.

CHAPTER FOUR

See Ya

The fourth picture, the one that she recognized, was less than a mile from her house, just up the block from the drugstore. It was the dirty, smelly, old alley that didn't go anywhere; she recognized the dumpster and the overflowing trash cans and the stagnant puddles. It was almost like a photograph was taken of it. She didn't remember a door being there though, especially a creepy shadow door, and she thought for sure she would have remembered that.

Chance looked out the window. It was Tuesday morning and the rain from the day before had stopped, but a thick white fog hung about the town. Her mom and dad both had to go to work, and it was still weeks before she had to start school so she had the whole day to herself—perfect for some real exploring to be had.

Even though it was summer, the weather had made it really cool, and she knew it was better to be slightly overdressed so she pulled on a pair of jeans with holes perfectly positioned in the knees and a faded out black shirt with a cute little ninja teddy bear drawn on the front. She slid on her red waterproof top boots and put on her sky blue coat with a hood, and slipped her arms through the straps of a backpack that was packed so perfectly that a Boy Scout would be proud—with a name like Chance she had to be prepared for anything the world could throw at her.

She went downstairs and found her mom waiting for her in the kitchen.

Her mom gave her a quick once over and took a sip of her coffee with just the slightest *humph* under her breath. "Something interesting is about to happen huh?"

Chance shrugged. "Seems that way, I found some old pages from a book with a picture on one of them I recognize. I have some exploring to do."

Like Chance, her mom knew too well to argue with fate, and didn't push the girl. "If something interesting is about to happen, I suppose you want to be right there in the middle of it."

Chance nodded.

Her mom sighed. "You'll be careful... right, and not do anything crazy?"

Chance smiled back.

She turned to the cupboard and picked out some energy bars, a bag of trail mix, a nice hunk of brownie that was still chewy, a bag of potato chips, and some nasty beef jerky as an emergency. She stuffed her supplies into her backpack along with a few energy drinks she had also taken from the refrigerator and zipped it closed. "I don't plan on doing anything stupid...

or at least I'm certainly going to try and not do anything stupid."

"Well do your best and just make sure you *try* to stay out of trouble, that's all we can ask," said her dad who must have entered the kitchen without her noticing

Chance finished off her orange juice and slid her arms through the straps of her backpack and headed for the door with her mom and dad both at her heels. She pulled the hood of the coat up onto her head and she went out.

She only made it about halfway down the steps when her dad caught up with her and for no reason at all he picked her up and spun her in a circle and set her back down. "Please be careful little girl."

Chance smiled and gave her dad a big hug. "I will… I promise."

Her dad walked back up the stairs and joined her mother. She waited until both of them stood framed in the doorway and waved goodbye. "Tell us all about it when you get back," said her dad, as they both grinned and waved back.

Chance leaped over the last two steps and hit the sidewalk running, quickly disappearing into the fog.

CHAPTER FIVE

Little Doors

Chance found the alley exactly as she remembered it, dirty and smelly with overflowing trash bins and murky, rubbish-filled puddles. She walked to the end of the alley and found exactly what she had seen before, a bricked up wall with no doors or strange shadows that looked like doors. She ran her hand over the wall, poking her fingers into all the little holes she could find and tracing them across the grout lines, then pushing and pulling on every brick, searching for the secret lever or switch that might trigger some elaborate clockwork that would release the mechanism to the hidden door.

For nearly fifteen minutes she looked and looked, but she couldn't find anything that would make the secret door appear.

Chance stepped back from the wall and slid her arms out of the straps of her backpack and dumped it on the cleanest patch of ground she could find on the alley floor. She rummaged through the contents and removed the crinkly yellow pages and flipped to the one with the picture of the alley. It was the right alley; the garbage was in all the correct places, the mist clung to the trash cans the same way, the puddles with the trash floating in them were there, everything in the picture pretty much matched up with this alley. But the alley she was in didn't have the little black shadow door—of course that is until she looked up from the picture to the actual alley wall, and this time it was there.

She laid down the pictures and stood up to examine the door, but the door was no longer there.

"*Erghhh*", said Chance out loud. She walked over to the wall to examine it better, but the door was still gone. Fairly annoyed she stepped back to her backpack and picked up the pages, and as soon as she flipped to the one with the alley in it, the door reappeared.

Both the door and the doorknob were black, and if she hadn't known better, it could easily have been overlooked as just another shadow. Chance hefted her backpack on to her shoulders and tightened the straps with one hand while holding the crinkly yellow pages with the alley picture on top in her other hand. She put her hand on the doorknob and turned it, and pushed open the door.

It opened into nothing but darkness. A cold wind blew in her face that smelled musty, and old. Chance stepped through the door and was in the utter absence of light. It was terrifying and exciting all at once, and she continued forward putting one foot in front of the other, but not totally sure if she was actually moving forward or not. There were no sounds—nothing at all—not of her footfalls as she walked or her heart beating in her chest or her lungs inhaling and exhaling as she breathed in and out… it was complete and absolute silence. She reached down to touch the ground, but couldn't feel anything, it was as if the darkness had solidified and she could somehow walk on it, and yet she continued putting one foot in front of the other crossing through the nothingness.

And then there was light, and she stepped through the doorway right back into the alley she started in, but it was not quite right. It was night time, and an overhead street lamp turned on, illuminating the mist and fog that still clung to the ground and walls in an eerie light. The light on the streetlamp started to flicker then suddenly exploded and electrical energy swirled like blue snakes hissing and slithering around the pole sending sparks in all directions. Then it got weird… really, really weird as if walking through solidified darkness wasn't weird enough. First the trash in the alley started moving around and reappearing and disappearing, then it was gone entirely and the bricks of the alley wall started to change color as if the years of soot and dirt were washing away, then the walls themselves began to break apart, not crumble, but un-build themselves first brick by brick then faster so that entire sections disappeared until the building was gone and she was standing in a deserted field of yellow, brown wheat and grain. A second later a wooden building was surrounding her, but as soon as she recognized it for what it was it melted away into nothing. Then she was in another field, but this time of beautiful wildflowers, but an instant later is was gone as well, and then she was in a marsh, then a swamp, then only recognizable for a millisecond she was under an ocean, and then it was all gone, and she was in space surrounded by a billion, billion stars spiraling outward, expanding away from a golden light so bright she had to shield her eyes from it. But soon everything faded again and new shapes began to form around her, first quickly, then slower and slower until time caught up and she was standing on solid ground in a strange new place that felt very different. She could breathe and hear and see and smell and she was pretty sure could taste because the air left bitterness in her mouth that wasn't at all pleasant, but there existed no question that this was not the same place she left, nor was this any place on her world.

It felt old, very, very old, and menacing.

CHAPTER SIX

This Isn't Kansas Any More

The first thing Chance noticed was the light, an odd shade of gray with the slightest hint of orange and a bit of purple around the edges. It was the kind of light that occurs just a moment after the sun sets, when the sky fills in with grey just before it gets dark. The second thing she noticed was that she was standing in a glade at the edge of a forest, but on closer inspection the trees of that forest weren't really trees, or at least the kind of trees she was used to seeing. They were big and tall and solid looking, but they really looked more like giant mushrooms with large dull red splotches which would probably be much brighter if the sky didn't cast them in grey-orange light.

Chance found a stick on the ground and

walked up to one of the mushroom trees and poked it. She expected it to be soft and squishy like a mushroom in her world, but it wasn't, it was hard and unforgiving just like the bark of a tree, and the closer she looked, the more it did look like a tree. There were branches under the hood of the mushroom instead of the gills that you would typically see, and the hood wasn't actually a hood at all, but thousands of smaller branches with dark leaves packed so tightly together that they looked solid just like a mushroom top, and the red splotches were actually some kind of fungus that blossomed out in tight swirls with a smooth slightly shiny look about them.

There were real trees in the glade as well, but they were much uglier than the trees she was used to seeing. They had dark, hard trunks and tiny black leaves with only the slightest hint of green running in thin veins over their surface. She noticed other types as well, some tall, some short, some fat and others round, but none of them looked particularly pleasant to the eye. They weren't exactly repulsive, nor could they be called attractive, but something foreign and strange and difficult to describe. The forest surrounded her and the trees were grouped too close to see far ahead. Chance would have liked to have climbed up one, but she found that the branches were too high up for her to reach. She was stuck on the ground.

It occurred to her that she better try and find the doorway back to her world, but when she turned to see if it was in the middle of the glade, where it had been a moment before, it had disappeared. She held up the crinkled yellow pages and turned round and round, but no doorway appeared. She placed the pages back in her backpack and zipped them up and removed them again, but still no doorway.

Chance was only a little frightened that the doorway didn't reappear. If it had reappeared she would probably just walk right back through it and not properly investigate this strange new place for fear that the door wouldn't be there when she returned. But because it wasn't there, she had no excuse not to explore. She knew she should be afraid, but right now being afraid wouldn't get her home so she pushed those dark thoughts aside and decided that she could be afraid some other time when it was more convenient.

CHAPTER SEVEN

The Path

Chance decided that the grey-orange light was very annoying. It was just dark enough so she couldn't see everything in detail, but just light enough that she didn't immediately need more light. She decided it was best to play it safe and removed a flashlight from her pack anyway, but didn't turn it on so she could save the batteries for when she really needed it. It was long and black and made of aluminum so it was light and not a burden to carry, but it could also be used to knock somebody, or something, over the head with if necessary, but she hoped it would never come to that.

Chance walked the length of the glade, trying to find a way into the forest. She did find a path, but realized that finding a path meant that other people or creatures, or more likely both, used this path and they might not be at all happy to find her. In hopes of answers, she pulled off her backpack and rummaged through the contents to find anything that might be of use, but decided the flashlight was still about the best thing. She grabbed the flashlight and tightened her fist around the handle until her knuckles turned white and then with a deep breath stepped onto the trail and walked into the forest.

The ground was fairly level, so she easily followed the path as it wove its way through the forest between the strange ugly trees, and the giant mushrooms-like trees, and past odd-looking plants with dark purple flowers that gave off an unpleasant odor, and through vines that hung from the trees in dull green and red tumbles. She hiked over patches of crunchy grass that was a drab shade of puce and through drifts of dried-up black and pale yellow leaves and up a low ridge and down a shallow gully and through a copse of leafless white trees that resembled the bones of some great dead beast.

Up until this point something had been nagging at Chance. It wasn't that she had been walking for hours and hadn't come across anything alive; honestly she wasn't ready to meet up with anything alive yet anyway. It wasn't that since she arrived in this place the strange and annoying grey-orange sky hadn't changed either; it had not gotten lighter or darker or greyer or more orange or anything, it just stayed exactly the same shade of grey-orange that it was when she first arrived. It was none of those things, and that just annoyed her more.

So she continued to follow the path, looking for clues as to where she might be when she realized that the path disappeared into a large rockslide that must have tumbled down from the slope above her. At first she was afraid that she might have lost the path, but after a little searching, she found it again and was just about to start back into the woods on the other side of the rockslide when somewhere in front of her something howled.

Chance stopped in her tracks and waited and listened.

Howl!

That was the second howl, and it sounded closer. One howl in the distance is a bad thing, a second howl that sounds like its getting closer is a very bad thing, and Chance did what any sensible girl would do... she ran in the other direction.

She was scared, but it wasn't the kind of scared she was used to. This fear was a different sensation all together—and that made her even more scared.

Chance stopped at the edge of the rockslide and listened. She could see and hear things now in the forest and in the rocks around her—little black rabbit-like things with long ears and big feet, and brown squirrel-like things with bushy tails and big green eyes, and the commotion of birds as they took flight out of the ugly trees, and they were all running and flying away, and she knew it wasn't because of her. Whatever it was that howled had scared these creatures, and they knew enough to run, and she did too because whatever it was coming toward her was coming fast.

She knew it must be getting close because the forest went deathly silent again and she was getting desperate for a place to hide, but she could only find a small opening beneath some logs which must have fallen during the rockslide. Frantic, Chance crawled as far back as she could, hoping whatever it was would pass her by. She pushed herself as deep into the hollow as she could; pressing her back into the rocks and hoping she was thoroughly out of sight.

Chance could hear its footsteps getting louder as it drew nearer and nearer until it stopped just over her head on the logs above her. It snorted through its nostrils and she could feel the warm air from its breath as it drifted down through the logs of her hiding spot. It started to snuffle and slowly move back and forth over the logs spilling little rocks and pebbles over the ledge which clunked and thumped and rolled down the hill in front of her, but she didn't move and hardly breathed for fear it might hear her. She had no idea what it was above her, but every bone in her body was telling her to stay quiet, and that the thing above her was very bad indeed.

For a long tense moment she huddled in the back of the little cave under the fallen logs as the creature paced back and forth above her, sniffing and scratching and clawing at the wood. It circled back and forth from one end to the other, then slowly began to inch its way closer to where she was hiding, and she could see its shadow growing bigger and bigger. Its snuffling became more focused, and she knew it was at the edge of the log just above the lip of the opening. She was trembling and she knew it was only seconds before it found her.

But that moment never came.

Something changed; it straightened upright and growled, like a beast of prey, angry and frustrated. Stepping back from the ledge, the darkness retreated, and Chance could hear it running away from her hiding spot.

Chance quietly stuck her head out from the hole just to make sure it had really gone and wasn't just waiting to creep up on her when she wasn't looking. She looked around, but realized she didn't even know what she was looking for. She was a bit nervous to leave the cave, but the sensible part about her said that if she stayed, the creature might end up coming back, and if it did, that would be the first place it would look, so she crawled out and clambered back up the hill where she was able to pick up the path and follow it back into the forest.

52

CHAPTER EIGHT

Silver Eyed Fox

The trees in the forest on the opposite side of the rock slide weren't packed together as tightly so that she could see if something was coming, and that made her feel a little better.

Chance followed the winding path through the woods and for a while kept looking back over her shoulder to make sure nothing was following her even though the forest had remained silent since the creature had run off, but she still checked every few minutes just in case, because it is easier to be afraid of something you cannot see.

She kept walking, and then walked some more.

For the next few hours, nothing happened as she continued down the twisting path through the trees. She was getting hungry and tired, so she decided she would need to look for a safe place to rest soon. But as she walked on a little further the trees began to thin, enough that she could see that she was nearing a clearing, and for a moment worried that she might have walked in a full circle. When she broke through the tree line, she knew right away that she hadn't been there before and quickly forgot all about being tired and hungry and looking for a place to rest because things were just about to get strange or even stranger.

It was a large field covered in a dry, almost lifeless-looking brown grass that undulated slightly like the wind was blowing on it, but she couldn't feel any breeze. There was a smattering of the ugly trees and more of the mushroom-like trees, and a few big round rocks and quite a few smaller flat rocks that seemed to create a path through the field, but there were also new trees that for all intent and purpose looked dead.

Something was nagging at Chance again as she stared at the field trying to decide what to do next. It wasn't quite the same feeling she had when she heard the creature howl, it was more like something was watching her. She looked around and around to try to see who was there, but she didn't see any danger so she pushed the feeling aside and studied the flat rock path as it wound through the field from one side to the other. She looked behind her and realized that the path through the trees joined up to these steppingstones which made her think there was a reason for this step stone path to be here, and it would probably be a good idea to stay on it .

Chance stepped onto the first stone, which she learned too late was actually very slippery. She fell backwards, scraping her hand on a jagged section of the rock, dropping her flashlight, and landing very uncomfortably on her behind. Painfully, she rolled over on to her knees and bent her head down and put her eye up close to it to give it a better look. It was somewhat transparent, like black quartz, but it didn't seem to reflect any light and she realized that's why it hadn't looked smooth or slippery. She grabbed her flashlight, which fortunately was very tough and had only gotten a small scratch in it, and picked herself back up massaging her aching behind, and took another step forward—but this time a little slower.

Carefully Chance walked to the end of the first stone and realized the next one was too far away to reach and, still sore from her last lesson, didn't want to jump for fear of slipping and falling again. She stood there staring at the strange grass, trying to figure out what to do.

For the most part it looked like ordinary grass, just a bit thicker and softer looking, and maybe a bit drier, the way it would in the winter. It didn't look very dangerous, but something was telling her it was, so she turned and walked back into the forest to find a good, long stick.

She quickly found one that was a little more than three and a half feet long and wide enough for the end of her fingers to almost touch together when she grasped it. She took her flashlight and slid it into a little sling on her belt so that she would still have a free hand, wrapped her fingers around her new hiking stick, and walked back to the end of the first flat rock… right up to the edge.

Gently Chance poked the stick into the grass expecting it to touch ground, but it didn't, instead a ripple spread out from around the stick, just like dropping a stone into calm water, and expanded outward into the field. When the ripple passed under one of the dead looking trees, its shadow erupted in a flurry of flapping black wings, and what she thought had been leaves leaped from the branches and took flight and flew away. She looked up into the dead tree and into the grey-orange sky, but she couldn't see any birds in the sky, but when she looked back down into the field, she could still see the shadow birds flying away over the grass.

Chance pushed the stick into the grass to see if she could find the bottom, but it was deeper than the stick was long, and she really wasn't going to reach her hand or arm down into whatever this grass was just to see just how deep it would go. As she pulled the stick back up, she stirred it round and round in circles like it was a mixing bowl and she thought it had about the same consistency as cold cereal when all that is left is the soggy bits, but when she pulled the stick out it was surprisingly dry.

Chance looked at the long stone path ahead of her and all she could do was take in a deep long breath and sigh. She took her hiking stick and poked at the grass in front of the flat rock she was on, and after a few unsuccessful attempts, was very happy to hear a solid clunk. So she did it again and again, and determined that there was another smaller stone between the two flat rocks that was just under the surface of the grass, and she could use it to cross the gap that was too wide to jump. Very slowly she reached out her leg as far as it would go and probed the smaller stone with her foot to see if it would hold her weight which, to her great relief, didn't shift or rock back and forth or wobble and wasn't even very slippery. So she pushed off with her back foot and stood there between the two rocks in the grass that just covered the tops of her feet.

She did this over and over again, each time finding a smaller rock between the larger flat rocks if the big ones were too far apart to jump, and was able to make it midway through the field only slipping a couple of times, but not hurting herself or falling into the lake-o-grass which she had, incidentally, determined was a good name for it.

About midway across the field, Chance

found a fox. The fox was rusty red on top with white underparts and a long bushy tail with a white tip. It had big bright silvery eyes and a truly miserable expression on its face. It also just happened to be hanging upside down by its tail a few feet over the grass; the strange thing was that there didn't appear to be anything holding onto its tail so actually the fox appeared to be just magically hovering a few feet over the grass, upside down, with its tail straight up in the air.

"Hello," said Chance.

The fox limply raised one eyebrow and looked up at the girl. "Hello little girl."

Chance stared back at the fox.

It was a male voice and Chance could hear it in the back of her head. She turned round and round but no one was there except for the fox. "Did you just say something?"

"Assuming you're not just my imagination… I suppose I did," said the fox.

"How can you talk?" asked Chance. "I've

never heard a fox speak before."

With half interest the fox lifted its head a bit higher to get a better look at the girl. "Maybe you just haven't been listening."

"I'm fairly certain foxes don't speak where I'm from."

"We don't?" said the fox.

"No you don't," but she wavered for a moment. "Well I suppose, maybe, I just never tried to hear if they had anything to say."

"Maybe," said the fox.

Chance waved her hiking stick over the fox's tail in little circles but couldn't find any string or line or anything that was holding him up, and then she gave him a gentle jab in the backside just to make sure he wasn't just a trick.

"Ouch!" said the fox twisting around and waving its paws. "Hey watch out with that thing... that hurt." The fox's whiskers straightened and it gave the little girl renewed interest. "Frozen hairballs... that actually did hurt, you really are there aren't you?"

Chance looked slightly befuddled. "Well of course I'm here, where else would I be?"

"This isn't a hallucination?" said the fox.

Chance sighed. "I certainly wish it were a hallucination or bad dream, but I really don't think it is."

"If you're real, then where did you come from, and how did you get here?" said the fox with real interest. "And maybe if you are real, and I'm still not convinced you are, this might be just some kind of cruel trick—so tell me who sent you? Wait, I know… it was the Pixie wasn't it, all happy, smiling woodland sprite on the outside, but nothing but black-hearted rage on the inside," said the fox.

"Hmm, all right then, seems we may have a few issues to work out," said Chance as she slipped her arms out of the backpack straps and sat the pack down on the rock and opened it up. She rifled through its contents until she found the crinkly yellow pages with the picture of the alley on it and she held it up for the fox to see and then realized he was upside down so she flipped the pages over and held it in front of his eyes. "I'm from here." She twisted her head as far upside down as she could so she could properly look him in the eye, and pointed to the alley and the back wall. "I came through a funny little door on this brick wall at the end of this alley and ended up in this place. This peculiar place with all its giant mushroom things, and ugly trees, and nasty smelly flowers, and annoying grey-orange sky that never changes, and howling monsters that chase after you, and fields that look like grass but are actually lakes, and dead trees with shadows that shouldn't be there and then fly away, and all kinds of other things that I haven't been able to sort out yet."

The fox looked at the girl. "You're one very lost little girl aren't you?"

Chance sniffled and rubbed her sleeve

across her eyes, but managed to hold back most of the tears. "Yes… yes I am."

The fox went slightly rigid. "Little girl, did you say something about a monster?"

"Well I technically didn't see it, but I knew it was there," said Chance and she told him the story of how she had hidden under the logs when the creature came looking for her, and the fox listened intently, but didn't say anything until she was finished.

The fox crinkled its nose and scrunched up its eyes and Chance thought that he must be working something out in his head because it took him longer than it should to reply. "It sounds like a Hunter must have smelled you, but I've never heard of one losing the trail… once they get your scent, you are as good as d…," the fox looked into the little girl's sad eyes before finishing its thought, "well, I just never heard of one losing its quarry, it just doesn't happen, and they don't give up very easily."

"Well that's what happened. …So do you believe me now?"

The fox nodded. "I suppose I do, or at least I don't have any better options, do I?"

"Now if I get you down, then maybe you can help me get home," said Chance.

"Look, I doubt the Hunter is too happy that it lost you, and I'm pretty certain it won't happen again, so you had better get me down before it realizes its mistake and circles back around and finds us just hanging around chatting. Now if you want to get back home I might be able to help, but I have a request."

"What's that?" asked Chance.

"I want to go back with you," said the silver eyed fox.

"Can you really help?"

"Yes. Now please get me down from here, my tail hurts."

Chance looked at the fox that appeared to be magically hanging in midair. "I don't mean to sound too rude, but before I get you down should I know why you're up there in the first place?"

Howl!

Something far in the distance howled and both Chance and the fox went stiff.

"How about we just worry about getting me down first, we can get to that later," said the fox.

"Right," said Chance, "but I have no idea how."

The fox spotted the flashlight on her belt and grinned showing off its gleaming white teeth and extraordinarily pink tongue. "Is that a flashlight?"

Chance looked perplexed but pulled the big black flashlight with long aluminum handle from her belt and showed it to the fox. "Why yes it is and a real good one too."

"Excellent," said the fox, his big silver eyes gleaming, "now that will help considerably."

"All right, little girl, let's get this over with. Look through your shadow's eyes and cut the snare with your flashlight," said the fox. "But please be careful, from the looks of that thing it could probably slice me clean through if you slip, and you better be ready with that stick, I won't last a second if I fall into the lake, they're hungry down there."

"Who's shadow? How, exactly, am I supposed to use my flashlight to cut you down. I don't see anything. I think, maybe, you've been hanging there too long."

"I was afraid of that... you really have no idea what I'm talking about do you?"

Chance provided him a twisted smile back. "Bingo."

Howl!

The fox's ears twitched and it screwed up its face. "It's getting closer; we really don't have time for this."

"Time for what?"

"Look I will explain everything when we find a safe place to hide, now just close your eyes and listen to me," said the fox.

Chance didn't particularly like taking orders from an upside-down fox, especially one that she just met, but she also didn't particularly want that creature to find her again either so she did as he asked.

"Good, now stay still for a moment while I speak to your shadow, and hold your questions, it will all make sense real soon."

She could hear the fox whispering something, but she could only hear snippets of what he was saying and that made her think this may be some kind of joke. Then she began to feel funny and the very edges of her toes began to tingle and twitch. Then the sensation began to intensify to the point where it felt like millions of little needles were prickling and poking at her as it began spreading through her feet, then up her legs and past her knees and through her stomach, and then up through her spine until it slammed into her head and her whole body began to quiver and shake. Then suddenly with a *pop* it felt like her insides had been sucked right out of her and she staggered backwards from the force of it.

She could hear the fox in her head, but it didn't sound like he was talking to her, but at the same time she knew he was, and he was telling her not to open her eyes yet—so she didn't. But while she was standing there totally scared in this utterly bizarre world, the little gears in her head were still whirling and spinning round and round.

It was simple actually, and she knew it to be true with utter and total certainty, even though her brain was telling her it was impossible—it was her shadow, and it was alive, and she had been feeling its emotions all day.

Chance's eyes were still shut tight and she knew if she opened them everything would be different, she didn't know how she knew this, but she did, and she believed it. Then she heard the fox speaking again, and he told her to take a deep breath and relax, and to slowly open her eyes.

CHAPTER NINE

The Place Between Night And Day

It was black.

Then the world capsized, or maybe it wasn't the world, but rather she did, but she wasn't falling or hanging upside down like the fox and she didn't feel dizzy or really disoriented, but it did feel wrong, and reversed.

Shapes began to materialize in front of her, but it wasn't getting brighter, it was getting darker, even blacker if that was even possible. There were sounds as well, rustling, scurrying, wings flapping, wind blowing, water flowing, all the things that she realized had been missing from this world, but should have been there all along. As the darkness got deeper and deeper the clearer everything became until she could see everything around her, and it was beautiful and impossible all at once.

Everything was black, but she could see perfectly, the fox's shiny fur, his crooked whiskers, and his sharp claws. She could see the tree that the fox was hanging from with a snare wrapped around his tail, and all the little details she hadn't seen before, like the little leaves and big leaves and round ones and star-shaped ones, she could see even the tiniest things like the rough, striated bark on its trunk, and the little bugs wriggling and carving tunnels through it. She could see birds and clouds flying and drifting across the sky that was no longer grey-orange but whirling and swirling and indescribable, and long cracks and fissures in the shiny rock beneath her, and the field of grass was no longer a field but a lake, and everything was rich and vibrant and full of color, but it wasn't color it was black—the absence of color.

These colors she saw didn't exist. Yet somehow she could see them and understand that they were colors and that they were dazzling, and that thousands and thousands of varieties were all around her and these were all part of a color spectrum that couldn't be possible. Chance looked down and saw her shadow, but it wasn't her shadow it was her in full color—her colors—just like she would look in a mirror, and when Chance waved her hand she waved back.

"Yes, wow, everything is amazing, blah, blah, blah… now get me down before we're both dead."

Chance turned to the fox, "This is unbelievable. You're going to explain all this to me right?"

"Yes. Now turn on the flashlight, but be very careful and don't touch the beam."

Chance pressed the switch on the flashlight and a blazing beam of white light burst from lens and formed a blade of energy. "Whoa, that is so cool."

"Be careful and cut the snare."

With one hand Chance held the hiking

stick out under the fox so he wouldn't fall in the field of grass, that wasn't grass but a lake, and with the other hand she swung the flashlight beam through the snare cutting through it like butter. The fox dropped onto the stick but Chance couldn't hold its weight and she dropped him into the lake, and this was not the kind of lake you fell into and got out again.

The water boiled and splashed as tentacles broke through the surface twisting and wriggling and winding round and round racing toward the fox all barbs and hunger.

Chance grabbed for the stick but a tentacle had already wrapped itself around the yowling fox, she fought against it but it was too strong and it was pulling him under the surface, then in desperation she waved the flashlight's beam across the surface of the water striking the tentacle and shearing it in two spraying ooze into the air and covering the fox. Chance yanked the stick out of the water and heaved it and the fox onto the rock next to her in a heap of sticky glop.

The fox looked up at the girl its eyes still wide with fright. "That was miserable."

Chance grinned. "You're welcome."

Howl!

"I think he's found your scent, we need to go… now!" said the fox.

Chance nodded but didn't reply. She switched off her flashlight and slipped it into her belt then picked up the hiking stick in one hand, and grabbed the fox with the other. Unfortunately the fox was covered in slime, and she dropped him almost immediately, but he landed on his feet because he was a fox after all.

"Come on hero, just follow me," said the fox as he trotted ahead leaping from one flat rock to another, using his claws to keep him from falling.

In a couple of strides Chance caught up. Seeing through her shadows eye, she could make out the smaller submerged stones between the large ones and was able to keep pace with the fox. She followed him from one stone to the next, all the while resisting the urge to look up, forcing herself to ignore the new sounds and smells and sights that were overpowering all of her senses. She could feel the wind blowing over the water and it brought with it new scents that stunk and reeked and were lovely and pleasant and everything in between. She could hear the beating of bird wings far above and the churning and roiling of the lake water as a huge school of devilish looking fish swam only inches away. Yet somehow she resisted looking at all this for anything more than a glimpse.

They crossed from stone to stone until they'd reached the edge of the lake. There they found another path into the forest.

The fox raced on ahead hardly slowing. "Come on, move faster. There's a safe place to hide not too far from here."

Howl!

Chance didn't respond… she didn't need to.

The creature looked into the Technicolor sky and howled. The quills on its back jittered and it turned its head in the direction of the path seeing it as shades of colored heat, searching for a trial to follow but nothing was there—everything was cold. Then its nose twitched and it turned its head to the ground snuffling at the dirt, circling back and forth not exactly sure which direction to go, but he had the scent now; it was sweet and tangy, and smelled like fear… he was getting closer.

Chance and the fox ran along the forest path. They raced as fast as they could for longer than Chance had ever run before, and at last she dropped to her knees panting and exhausted.

When the fox realized the girl had stopped, it came back and seated itself next to her with its rough tongue dangling from the side of its mouth and his chest heaving in and out. "You know we really don't have time to rest."

Chance's head lifted slightly, and she clutched her side. "Can't run anymore...."

"We're not very far now; we can walk the rest of the way, and you can rest later when we're safe."

Chance nodded and stood up on wobbly legs.

"Follow me," the fox said, "we're going to leave the path so stay close behind me and do exactly what I say."

The fox found a break in the trees, and they carefully picked their way through the woods avoiding the withering and interlaced roots that covered the forest floor. The ground was rising slightly and the trees seemed to be getting thicker and taller and more ominous, which gave Chance the uneasy feeling that they were looking down and watching them. Looking ahead, she could see only tree-trunks of countless sizes and shapes. They were straight, bent, leaning, squat or slender, smooth or gnarled, and packed so close that many were curled and entwined around each other, and all of them were covered in moss and slime and shaggy growth.

For nearly two hours Chance followed behind the fox as they walked through the woods, splashing through cold clear streams and leaping over logs that had long since decayed and rotted through. The dense canopy kept the light dim and a thin mist clung to the trees which made it look a bit spooky, and the feeling that they were being watched was still there. The forest floor was blanketed in a thin shaggy fungus with a spattering of long-leafed fern-like plants which made it easy to walk. But where the canopy above opened, the undergrowth grew unchecked and they had to shove their way through tangled shrubs that looked like hemlock and fire-weed, and nettles and thistles, but probably wasn't. The deeper they went, the quieter it got, and Chance imagined she could hear whispering in the branches, and the uncomfortable feeling that they were being watched was getting worse until she found herself looking up and around and glancing back over her shoulder as if something was about to jump out at her at any moment.

Chance started to wonder if the fox knew where he was going and was about to say something when she realized the trees were thinning and the path became easier to follow. Then suddenly they broke free of the woods and found themselves at the edge of an enormous ring of giant mushroom trees. The fox looked back at the girl and smiled as if he knew exactly what she was thinking.

"What? I didn't doubt you for a second," said Chance.

The fox walked to the center of the fairy

ring, and turned round in a full circle carefully studying each of the mushrooms. Chance counted thirty seven of them in all and each one was more than fifty feet tall and twice as wide. They were covered in delightful swirls and whirls of various colors that made no sense to her as she was still looking through her shadow's eyes, but she decided they must be alternate shades of red and blue and yellow because those would like nice, and because she had no names for these colors she decided all the colors would simply be alternate colors of something she knew.

"Come on... I've found what we're looking for," said the fox as he headed toward one of the towering mushroom trees. The tree had a band of different color whirls around the base of the stalk and the fox examined each one with interest. With his paw he touched one that wasn't blue (but could be) and then circled around the stalk one time to the left and touched the same whirl again, and when he did this a little arrow appeared above the alternate blue whirl. When he touched it again it turned a color that isn't green and then he circled around the stalk one full circle to the right and touched the whirl again and it changed to a color that wasn't red, followed by two more trips around the stalk once to the left and two more to the right each trip around generating a new color in the whirl below the arrow. On his last trip around, when he finally returned to the arrow, Chance heard a *click* and a small door opened on the stalk where there hadn't been one a moment before.

"Come on… we'll be safe now," said the fox and he stepped through the door and into the stalk of the giant mushroom tree.

Chance followed behind.

CHAPTER TEN

This Is Where We Are

There was a damp, musty smell, and for a moment she couldn't see anything, but as her eyes became accustomed to the darkness, she realized they were at the base of a circular staircase that was carved into the outer wall of the stalk and wound its way upward disappearing from view.

They walked up the stairs and through a trapdoor in the floor and into a large circular room with a domed ceiling and Chance decided that this is how she would have imagined the inside of a carved out mushroom would look like, but it was also more interesting than she thought it would be, and didn't smell bad in the least—which she thought it would.

Chance immediately liked the room. The walls were painted a color that wasn't yellow with large polka-dots, which could be purple but weren't, randomly splattered about. The domed ceiling was the color of the sky and seemed to change as if it was copying what the sky was doing outside, which happened to be darkening at the moment. The floor was covered in carpet that wasn't green and looked like it had been woven from moss, but was surprisingly soft to the touch. The whole room smelled like scented lilac candles, and foreign spices, cinnamon rolls and sanctuary. There was furniture in here as well, chairs and tables and foot stools and desks and lamps and an extremely comfortable looking couch that reminded her of how tired she was. There were extraordinary and bizarre and amazing things on the shelves and on the tables and hanging from the walls: glowing orbs filled with little flying creatures, potted plants that looked like little dragons that could actually breath fire (positioned away from the drapes), and a clockwork robot that wandered around the room trimming the moss carpet and collecting the occasional scorched bug that flew too close to the fire-breathing dragon plant. There was a bookshelf filled with round books, triangular books, and diamond-shaped books in languages that she couldn't read. There were rows of little liquid-filled bottles packed with strange roots, eyeballs, teeth, weird appendages, reptiles, fish and all types of other gross things. There was a shelf filled with miniature dinosaur-like skeletons that wandered back and forth apparently trying to get up the nerve to jump to the floor, but when one finally did it hit the ground and broke apart, and the clockwork robot picked up all the bones and reassembled them and put it back on the shelf so it could do it again. There were paintings on the walls showing fairies and pixies and elves dancing among the trees under a star-filled sky, and other paintings that watched you with beady little eyeballs and threw gobs of paint at you if you walked up to them, and a chair with teeth that wouldn't let you sit in it, and a fish bowl with a sea monster that had its tentacles wrapped around a model ship and was crushing and pulling it under the water while the tiny crew and passengers manned lifeboats and jumped for their lives overboard, and many, many more things that would take hours to discover.

"Silver eyed fox," said Chance as she sat down on the couch, "can you please tell me what this place is?"

The fox smoothly leaped onto a footstool at Chance's feet and began to groom itself. "I suppose it is that time," said the fox.

"So I don't even know your name… mine's Chance, what's yours?"

The fox's tail twitched, it stopped grooming itself, and it looked up at the girl its silver eyes sparkling. "Chance?"

"Yes. Chance Nancy Counter," said Chance.

The fox's whiskers rose and it smiled revealing pointy white teeth. *"Chance N. Counter,* now that is a fitting name… especially fitting for me today I would say."

Chance grinned back but didn't respond.

"We foxes have only ten different names, and mine is *Seven.* You can see it on the back of my neck."

Chance leaned forward in her seat and twisted her head around so she could get a better look at the back of the fox's neck. "That's an interesting name, and I'll be darned, the hairs on the back of your neck do look just like the number seven."

The fox's tail swooshed back and forth, and he watched the little girl. "Yes, just like the number seven. It's there when we're born; I guess it takes the work out of choosing a name," said the silver eyed fox named Seven.

Chance smiled. "I suppose it does."

"Now let me tell you what I know about where we are," said the fox as he circled around the footstool kneading at the cushion until he was satisfied enough to lie down and curl into a little ball. "This is the Place Between."

"Between what?" asked Chance.

"We are in the place between night and day. It lies just outside of our world, just outside of time, and most certainly outside of reality. It is the place where darkness and shadows come from. It is the place where nightmares and fairytales and monsters that live under your bed, and creatures that go bump in the night were created. This is the place of lore and legend and dreams, and the place where the Shadow King reigns supreme."

"How can there be a place between night and day... wouldn't that be just the moment between night and day?"

"Yes I suppose it would be that too," said the fox.

"So is it a place or a time?" asked Chance.

The fox's tail began flicking back and forth. "Both, it would not only be a place between night and day, but it would also be the moment between night and day."

"How can there be a place that is really a time?"

"Because, of course, it is a place that is stuck in time," said the fox like it should be totally obvious.

"Oh, I see," said Chance, but she really didn't.

The fox smiled and showed all his teeth.

Chance didn't see any point in arguing. "So do you live here?"

"No."

"Then how did you get here?"

"Same as you I suppose… through one of the doors. That old saying about how 'curiosity killed the cat'… it's the same for foxes."

Chance scrunched up her eyes. "So how can I find one that takes me back out?"

"Are you ready to leave already?"

"Yes, I think I've seen enough," said Chance.

"So have I," said the fox, "but getting out is the hard part. There are many ways in, but I only know one way out."

Chance said nothing; she didn't have to, the fox knew exactly what she was thinking.

"Right, this place has been around since the beginning of time, long before humans huddled in caves terrified of the night, long before the dinosaurs walked the Earth, and the fish swam in the sea… it goes all the way back to the beginning, right when the very first night became day."

"So how does this help me get home, and how do you know so much about this place if you aren't from here?" said Chance with maybe a bit too much skepticism.

"I've been here for a while, and I know what I know from listening and reading and asking questions when I know it is the time to ask questions."

Chance blushed. "I apologize, Seven, please continue."

"Time does not exist here, so the world can be doing what it pleases on the outside and has nothing to do with what is going on here. From the looks of your clothes I suspect I'm from your future, but I've been here long before you arrived," said the fox with a twisted smile. "It's all about perspective; the future is only the future to someone from the past. You think you live in the present, but to me you are from the past. In this place there is no future or present or past... there's just now. "

Chance stretched out her arms. "Then how can all this be... I mean how can anything be happening if it doesn't take time to happen?"

"Because it just does," said the fox. "This

is a *place* and for a place to be a place it has to change and grow and shrink and the cycle of life must go on and all these things need to happen or it really isn't a place at all, that's why. This is the home of the Shadow King and this what he likes, it is dangerous and beautiful and ugly and scary and strange and diabolical and endearing, and this is where he is strong, and this is how he wants it to be. Time is only a creation of man so that he can sequence and compare events like the sun traveling across the sky, or the swing of a pendulum, or the years of his life, or maybe it's just a way to sell watches. But here it does not matter, because in this place there is no time… the Shadow King has no need for it."

The fox wasn't finished, but he waited for Chance to catch up or ask a question, but she couldn't think of anything to say so he continued. "The Shadow King is the first of all shadows and all shadows since then are related to him, this is their home and this is their world and for that reason we must look through their eyes to understand this place and navigate through it. In this place we can see what they see, and if you look down at your shadow you will see how your shadow sees you."

Chance looked down at her shadow and saw herself like she was looking into a mirror. She touched her hand to the ground, but all she could feel was the soft mossy carpet. "That is so weird."

The fox frowned in a way that only an animal can. "Yes it is… I try not to look, it gives me the shivers. I want to leave this place, I've been trying to get out for a long time now, but without help I can't."

"This is just all so confusing that I don't know what to say or do—but I want to leave and I'll do what I can to help us both get out of here," said Chance.

The fox grinned, and was quiet for a moment. "Those pictures you showed me are from the *book*. It contains hundreds of pages filled with pictures of places where doors to this world can be found. But over the eons pages from the book have been lost, and The Shadow King is ever watchful for them so he can return them to the book where they belong. You uncovered some of those lost pages and used them to find a door to this place, and now you are stuck here as well. But you're not the first, there have been others and that's why we have safe places to hide from the Shadow King and his followers because he wants nothing more than to do away with us or feed us to his kin. But his Hunters are out there and they're looking for us and others like us who don't belong in this world and eventually they will find us and the Shadow King will have more pages for his book."

Chance gulped.

"The only way out of this place is through the Portal in the King's castle. That is where the book is and the place where we can access any door to any time and any place that the page of the book is turned to. We need to take your pages and put them back in the book and then we can open the portal to your home, and if we can do this we might have a small chance to escape… actually a very slim, really almost an impossible chance to escape, but there is that slight glimmer of hope I guess."

"Optimistic I see," said Chance.

"I am a fox, by nature we are not a very optimistic lot, now if I may continue?"

"Please, go right ahead."

"So to do this we will have to make our way through an ancient deep dark maze-like forest of whispering trees that forms a ring around his castle to keep trespassers out. The trees in that miserable wood listen to your thoughts and prey on your fears until you become hopelessly lost within its realm.

"If we make it through the woods, we

then have to cross over the only access to the castle, which happens to be a narrow, extremely well-guarded bridge. Finally, if we do manage to cross the bridge, hold on, did I mention that the castle is floating in the air above a bottomless pit? I probably overlooked that didn't I? Anyway, we will have to somehow find our way through the castle and into the portal room that is guarded by a half-starved vicious dog who lives half in the shadow world and half in our world and whose sole purpose is to...."

"To prevent anyone from using the portal that isn't supposed to," interrupted Chance.

The fox looked up at the girl. "Yes, it seems we are on the same page now."

Chance nodded. "Is there any other way to get home?"

The fox's tail twitched.

"When I first arrived, I was captured and taken to the castle to be an item on the dinner menu, incidentally a particular high honor I was told—but I managed to escape and hide in the castle's many passageways and hidden corners and deserted rooms. During this time I learned of the things I'm telling you now, and I'm familiar with the castle's layout and its workings. If there is another way into or out of that place I never heard, and believe me I tried.

There is something else, but I don't know if it can help us or not. The Shadow King uses his power to send shadows into our world to hide in the dark forests and deep caves and seedy alleys and behind blind corners and under beds and in the closets and cupboards so we never forget that there are strange and dangerous things still out there. But I learned that the Shadow King's influence on our world is weakening. Up through the Dark Ages he ruled the night, but it seems man is not as afraid of the darkness as he once was. The Shadow King has long been plotting and conceiving schemes to change this, but before I could learn more of what he was planning I was caught and only escaped with my life, and have been on the run ever since."

"It's amazing you're still alive, fox."

The fox's tail stopped swishing back and forth. "Please don't say that, it just isn't nice, to a fox it's like a horrible jinx. You might as well tell an actor good luck before going on stage, or a taxi cab driver he's such a good driver he'll probably never get in an accident."

"Humph. What do you know... a superstitious fox. But I'm sorry; I didn't mean it to be rude. You have to admit it is pretty amazing that you could have survived here for so long and still hang on to your sanity."

"Crazy like a fox," said the fox with a toothy grin.

Chance squirmed in her seat. "So what do we do now?"

"First we start by hiding out here until the Hunter has lost our trail. These hideouts are veiled from them, and they can't track us, so as long as we're in here we should be safe. We'll rest for the evening and get started in the morning. Each of the hideouts has a map to the next one, and we will use it to help us pass through the forest and decide our next move from there—assuming that we make it that far.

Chance slipped off her shoes and pulled her feet up onto the sofa and fell asleep before even realizing that she probably wouldn't be able to sleep.

CHAPTER ELEVEN

Shhh… The Trees Are Watching

Chance woke up to a beam of light shining in her face. She stretched out her arms and rubbed her fists into her eyes seeing only the quickly fading lightshow on the back of her eyelids and for a moment thought she had just awoken from a strange and tiresome dream. The moment passed quickly when she realized that she wasn't lying in her own warm, soft bed, and the light that was shining in her face was coming through a colorful glass swirl that was carved into the roof of a mushroom.

The silver eyed fox leaped up onto her lap and Chance scratched it behind the ears, which didn't seem to bother him at all. "I see you're awake. I probably let you sleep too long, but you seemed so peaceful I didn't have the heart.”

"Thanks, I didn't realize how tired I was."

"No problem, it will probably be the last real sleep you'll get for the next few days anyway."

Chance pushed the fox off her lap and shuffled over to a small door at the far end of the room that she hoped was a bathroom, and was very relieved when she opened it that it was, and that it functioned the way it was supposed to. By the time she had finished, the fox had already found a map and was studying it to figure out their next move.

"From the looks of this, we head north for about two hours and we will run into a small river that we can follow east and should lead us into the forest."

"So north, south, east, and west work the same way here?" asked Chance.

"Yes, and a compass works as well."

"Good, I just happen to have an excellent one so we won't have to borrow one," said Chance.

The fox turned back to the map. "It will take us about two days to reach the other side of the forest, and we have to make sure we are under cover by nightfall, because we wouldn't make it an hour after the nocturnal predators begin hunting. Fortunately the maps says that there is a small cave that we can hold up in for the night, but we'll have to keep up a good pace, since it will take us most of the day to get there."

Chance followed the fox's paw as he moved it across the map. "That little smiley face is the cave?" asked Chance who was looking at a little circle that should be yellow with two black dots and a curved line under them.

The fox smirked. "Yes that's how all of them are marked, but they aren't just plastered in plain sight you have to know what you're looking for."

Chance opened up her backpack and reorganized the contents realizing not anything in there looked quite like it did when she had packed them. "What's happened to all my stuff?" she asked the fox.

The fox jumped to the floor and examined the contents. "Oh everything is the same I'm sure… it's just the shadow of those things. Most of them will probably still work like they should."

Chance removed the compass or at least what she thought was the compass because it had a dial that moved when she rotated it and the letters N, S, E, and W printed on its face.

Her stomach growled, and she realized that she hadn't eaten in quite some time, so she reached her hand in the bag and removed a long rectangular bar that she hoped was a protein bar, and what she assumed was an energy drink, and a little clear bottle with a tube and pump handle on it which still looked pretty much the same as she thought it should. "I brought enough food for a couple of days, but I only have enough to drink for today. I have a purifier; if we filter the water can we drink it?"

The fox stuck his head in the backpack and scrounged around. "Wow… you really are prepared for just about anything, and yes the water is drinkable here, but filtering it wouldn't hurt. We can also eat certain fruits which actually taste pretty good, but let me show you what they are because the wrong ones can turn you into a jabbering fool."

"Nice to know," said Chance as she admired a square-shaped object that appeared to be food in a bowl on one of the tables.

The fox watched her as she dropped it back in the bowl. "Usually the square ones are safe; it's the round ones you want to stay away from."

"Thanks, I'll try to remember that."

The fox leaped from the table to the

couch and up to a windowsill where he looked out over the forest. "Looks like the coast is clear, and the longer we lounge around, the more daylight we are burning. We should get moving."

Chance zipped up her pack and slid it over her shoulders. "Ready as I'll ever be I suppose."

They opened the hatch in the floor of the room, and went out the door. Chance took a bearing on the compass, and the fox led the way into the surrounding woods. He brought them back to the edge of the path where he stopped, listened to the wind, smelled the air, and let his keen eyes peer down the path until he was satisfied they were alone.

"It's clear. Let's try to keep on the path for as long as we can. We should run into the river in a couple of hours at the most, and that's when the fun begins. Don't let your guard down; everything is out to get us around here."

Chance nodded, but didn't reply.

The two of them followed the path until it ran into a river with a stone bridge that crossed over it. They stopped and watched the river flow as a log drifted under the bridge carried along on the swift current until it disappeared from view as it turned a bend into the forest. The rivers in the Between are really no different than any other rivers, some flow north to south other east to west, and a few like the one they were standing before, flowed west to east carrying sticks, logs, assorted garbage, discarded junk, the occasional animal carcass, and other even less pleasant by-products of civilization.

This particular log they were watching, which had been a small tree growing at the edge of a lake hundreds of miles away, was cut down and subsequently lost by a beaver-like animal that really wasn't a beaver but looked like one because it had generally the same attributes. This beaver-like creature lost the log when a mountain lion-like creature which actually is akin to the present day mountain lion decided the beaver-like animal would make a good meal. The log fell into the lake and drifted into the river where on its passage eastward it floated by an abandoned ghost town, a small copse of mangrove-like trees where river rats lived in the roots, under a long iron bridge with ugly gargoyle statues, and past a series of lochs and waterwheels that provide power to the occasional barges and ramshackle houses that sporadically populate the riverbank. Then it traveled for another twenty miles of open plains before getting pulled from the water by a town of grizzly river folk who make their living from the things that drift by. After deciding the log wasn't of any value the river folk dumped it back in the flow where it drifted another hundred miles under the bridge that they are standing on and through the forest and out over a grand cascading waterfall that disappeared into the mist and fog and mystery of the bottomless pit.

From the bridge the fox watched the log disappear into the dark forest. "On dark and stormy nights when lightning flashes across the sky and horrifying shadows flash on the walls, it is these trees that you see. This forest is the source of those menacing shadows, all twisted and gnarled with nightmarish faces etched in the bark, and long strangling limbs that seem to have hands with knotted fingers ready to snatch you if you walk underneath them. Five minutes in there and you'll know why little boys and girls want to sleep with the lights on."

The fox held his breath for moment, his tail swishing with a mind of its own below him. "This just isn't a safe place for a fox and a little girl to go."

"No, it isn't," Chance agreed, as she skipped a stone into the river and watched as it sunk.

The silver eyed fox led Chance into the

forest under the huge branches of the trees. Mist gathered about them, and the only visible sunlight came from gaps in the dense canopy. It smelled of damp and decay of dirt and stone and ancient times. They followed the course of the river on a path of stones and roots that was too narrow for them to walk side-by-side.

They went with as much speed as the uneven ground and mud would allow, trudging on like this until mid-day, when they stopped and took a quick break for lunch and to rest.

"Let's have some water from the river while we have an opportunity and save the bottled drinks I brought along for later in case we need them," said Chance as she filled and pumped the river water through her purifier.

The water was clear and cold and the fox took a long drink from a little bowl that Chance had in her pack. "Not too bad… maybe there is some good to this place after all."

Chance took a long drink for herself and

listened to the forest. She could hear the trees whispering at an almost inaudible level, but there were definitely muffled voices on the air. "These talking trees give me the creeps; do you understand anything they are saying?"

The fox looked up at her and grinned humorlessly. "Yes I do. And no, you really don't," said the fox.

Chance took another drink of the cool water.

They continued deeper into the woods. The trees started to rustle in the upper canopy, the whispering was getting louder, and the further they walked the more oppressing it became as though the trees were trying to suck the life from them. Chance could hear what they were saying now, and it was troubling and horrifying—they had decided on their fate and it wasn't good. The voices were getting louder and louder and Chance was teetering on the edge of panic, but she remembered home and her parents, and that she needed to do this because if she didn't, she could never leave, and that to her wasn't an option.

The fox frowned. "We're about to have some company, switch on your flashlight."

Chance pulled the flashlight from her belt and, just as before, when she turned it on a brilliant beam of white light burst from the lens and took the shape of a blazing sword.

They could see it coming toward them still a good ways ahead. It was moving slowly, as though assessing the situation. Then another one appeared next to it, and their pace quickened. They looked like wild dogs, but weren't very big, maybe thirty or forty pounds. When they got a little closer, she thought they looked more reptilian with dark, smooth skin. One of them started running straight at them, mud and water splashed up from around its feet, and it leaped in the air directly at Chance with a wide-open mouth full of crooked teeth. Chance swung the flashlight around in a perfect arc and the gleaming blade of light sliced the creature in two, instantly vaporizing it in a spray of dissipating black mist. The second creature growled, but hesitated, still more than twenty feet away. Chance and the beast stared at each other across the gap for what seemed like an eternity, but when she thought it was about to attack it leaped away into the dense underbrush next to the path and into the forest. Chance turned off the flashlight and dropped it to the ground with a satisfying plop as it landed in the mud; she inhaled deeply and bent to her knees realizing she had been holding her breath the whole time.

"That was brilliant," said the fox.

"Were those Hunters?"

The fox didn't even look up. "Not even close, they weren't much more than a couple of wild shadow hounds. They usually travel in packs so I'm guessing they were just a couple of scouts. The next time we encounter them there will probably be more."

Chance glared at the fox.

"Right, good job, but let's get moving… we need to get to the cave before dark," said the fox as he pushed on down the path.

Chance grabbed the flashlight, put it back in her belt, stood up and followed him without saying a word.

For the next few hours it was quiet. Even the trees seemed to have silenced themselves. All that they could hear was the river rushing passed them, splashing over rocks.

As the day went by, Chance's nerves calmed, and she began paying more attention to her surroundings admiring the forest for its beauty even in its dark and sinister way. Many great trees grew there in thickets and groves and copses of what looked vaguely like oak, fir, pine, ash and aspen, but were different enough that she knew they couldn't be, and as they moved closer to the center of the forest she could feel their life-sucking pull again. Dark, thick moss grew on most of them, blanketing their roots and covering their bark. Some of the trees had faces of old weathered men and gnarled women, and she felt that they were watching her, even though she never saw their eyes move, but there was little question that she was a trespasser in these woods and they didn't want her there.

Occasionally thin streaks of light penetrated the thick canopy, and in those places the bushes and shrubs and plants and flowers and even the mushrooms grew with colorful markings and bright leaves and creeping vines that climbed over the rocks and up the trees stretching as far as they could go looking for the sun.

Next to the river, long reeds grew with round, bulbous pods like nautilus shells, and when she squeezed one of them a fine powdery dust blew out over the river which attracted a school of fish. But as she watched it drift off into the current, what Chance thought were roots snapped up from the ground and struck the water impaling the fish on barbed tentacles before stuffing them into a wide open maw in the mud at the river's edge that hadn't been there a moment before. Chance leaped away just as one of the tentacles turned to her and tore into her jacket ripping a gash in the fabric before she was able to yank it away.

"Let's try to keep our hands and feet to ourselves now," cooed the fox.

"Uh huh," nodded Chance.

The sky was getting darker and the mist was gathering about them again. The fox pushed them onward, following the river as it bent east and then north and then east again deeper into the woods. As the day grew darker they could hear what sounded like a wolf howl in the distance, and they quickened their pace.

"Hunter," said the fox with nervous expression on his canine-like face.

Chance unconsciously put her hand on the flashlight.

The ground had become firmer, and this made traveling less rocky, but it seemed that the night creatures were growing louder.

The trail opened up on a small clearing and in the clearing was a group of about fifteen cats, or at least they looked something like cats, just bigger with bobbed tails and long tufts of hair on their pointy ears. They had luxurious fur that wasn't gold, but something that could almost be that color with long dark stripes like a tigers. They were adorable and beautiful and irresistible, just looking at them made you want to pick one up and cuddle with it and pet its sleek fur that looked so smooth and soft and silky.

Chance was thinking that very thing when a herd of what could be enormous elk emerged from the forest. They were huge and daunting, bigger than any elk she had ever seen before, but when they saw the cats they went still like they were too scared to move even though they could probably crush one under a hoof and hardly notice.

One of the cats turned and spotted the elk herd and its eyes burned with a color that wasn't green and it made a soft yowling sound which made all the others turn as well. Then suddenly, as one, they rushed the herd so fast Chance could only see a streak of color flash across the clearing. The next was a sea of hooves and gold and flying tufts of hair and clumps of grass all balled up in a whirlwind of chaos. Methodically they went from one elk to the next leaving behind a pile of gleaming white bones and in only a matter of seconds they had devoured the entire herd.

"Move now," said the fox as he grabbed her by the pant leg and began pulling.

Chance was hypnotized by the madness she was watching, and only because the fox swatted her leg with his claws did he get her attention.

"We leave this place now, or we'll be next."

Chance nodded and they both crept back into the forest and skirted around the clearing and made it back to the trail without being noticed.

"They're like piranhas," said Chance when they had moved far enough away that she felt they wouldn't be heard.

The fox looked up at her. "That would be my cousin Jack and his family. Well, second cousin twice removed."

Chance smiled. "Humph."

By early evening, the mist had grown thicker, quickly becoming a wall of impenetrable gloom making it almost impossible to continue. They heard voices, whispering and groaning and the endless rustling of the woods around them, but just when hope was nearly lost, a shape began to appear in front of them, and they came to the edge of a small hill surrounded by a ring of boulders that was hardly discernable in the mist.

"This is it," said the fox. "Now we just have to find the door."

"What am I looking for?"

"Not exactly sure, the map didn't say, but let me know if you find it," said the fox quite uncertainly.

"That's just great."

A darkness crept about them, blacker than night. They searched each of the boulders one by one, but couldn't find anything that looked like a cave entrance, but then, from just over the tree line, a moon that wasn't silver sent a beam of moonlight that caught one of the boulders and illuminated a happy smiley face etched in the stone.

In three strides the fox leaped to the top of the boulder and studied the marking. "Use your finger and trace the circle of the face in a clockwise rotation."

Chance nodded and did as he said.

"Good, now place your finger first in the left eye, then the right, and finally trace the smile."

"OK," said Chance as she did what he requested.

As she completed the final swipe of the smile they heard a gentle *creak* and a thin beam of light illuminated the edge of a door on the interior face of two boulders that had been pressed closely together.

"We go down there," said Seven who had just pushed open the door revealing a narrow flight of stairs cut into the stone that led down into the darkness.

CHAPTER TWELVE

Not So Safe

Something big crunched through the woods no more than a few feet away, and Chance pushed the fox into the hole, then quickly followed behind him, but just as she pulled the door shut behind them something slipped through the crack. In the blackness they couldn't see what it was, but it moved astoundingly fast and disappeared down the stairs.

"What was that thing?" cried Chance.

"I have no idea, but whatever it is, it's down here with us."

Chance pulled her flashlight from her belt and clicked it on. She swung the beam around the stairwell illuminating the carved stone steps, and rock walls and ceiling, but there was nothing. With the flashlight in hand she cautiously led them down the stairs one step at a time.

The beam arced across the bottom of the stairs and briefly illuminated a rock floor. "We're just about at the bottom and we're coming out into some kind of room."

The fox eased its way beside her and they both hesitated on the last step. Chance pointed the flashlight into the open space slowly drawing the beam from one side of the room to the other. She got about half way when she heard a noise coming from the back wall; it was a scraping sound, like something was dragging or maybe slithering over pebbles.

She could feel the fox press up against her leg.

When she pointed the flashlight towards the sound she saw it for an instant before it hissed and disappeared. It was long and serpentine, and almost transparent, ghostlike, a color that wasn't black smoke, and it vanished before she could see anything else. Then something slammed into her leg and she screamed dropping the flashlight and tumbled off the bottom stair into the room. The thing had wrapped itself around her ankle and was trying to bite her leg, but its fangs weren't long enough to penetrate her boot and she managed to kick it off with her other foot, and when she did she knew it had disappeared again.

She staggered to her feet and was suddenly blinded when the lights in the room came on, and she realized she was no longer looking through her shadow's eyes because the light was dim and dull, and everything looked ordinary, and made sense. It was a relatively small room with a rocky floor and boring furniture that looked like it had been carved from the lifeless rock surrounding her. Her flashlight was at her feet still glowing, but was no longer the gleaming white blade of a sword, but just an ordinary beam hardly visible in the lit room. All she could see was the room, and the fox, and the furniture, but no creature.

Chance picked up the flashlight holding it like a sword and scanned the room. There was a table, and a chair and a couch, but not much else. She scrutinized the room from one side to the other, but nothing moved or was hiding in the corners or on the couch or under the table laying in wait. She turned to the shadows on the walls, but nothing looked out of the ordinary with them either.

"Seven, where did it go?"

The fox said nothing, but he didn't have to: he was watching the wall. The hair on his back was standing on end and his tail was flicking from side to side, and he looked like he was about to pounce, but Chance couldn't figure out at what. She thought to herself that this is exactly one of those times when an animal stares at something that doesn't appear to be there, it's creepy, and scary, and it makes you realize there is more to the world than you know.

She followed his gaze back to the shadow on the wall and realized the voice that was not quite in her head was telling her that, most of the time, tables don't have five legs. So she looked back at the real table and counted four legs, and then back to the shadow and counted five. She could swear she heard the little voice tell her 'I told you so,' but she really didn't care because the fifth leg of the shadow twisted around and turned towards her hissing, and when a shadow hisses it's very frightening, and other little things don't matter so much.

The snake-like shadow on the wall hissed again, and slithered away from the table, never lifting its gaze from her. It coiled back and struck, but as a shadow it was only two dimensional and didn't leap from the wall, but rather glided across the floor as a shadow would. She dodged to the side and it rushed past her. An instant later, she was thrown backwards, landing hard on her backside, and when she tried to get up she couldn't stand because her legs were stuck together, like they were bound, but nothing was binding them and whatever it was, was twisting its way up her body constricting and tightening its grip as it went.

The invisible assailant had made it half way up her chest sucking the air from her lungs and she tried struggling to break free, but that only made it worse. She felt it reaching for her arms pulling them in to her sides trying to immobilize her and she started to panic, but then she heard the fox yelling her name and trying to tell her something, and she realized he had been trying to get the flashlight into her hand. The part of her that lived in the normal world, the one where monsters weren't hunting her down, and where blue was really blue and it was the color of the sky was wondering how that would help, but the shadow part of her that was from this world knew it would and told her to look at her shadow, and finally she saw.

Chance saw the snake-like creature winding its way up her own shadow crushing it as it went, and she could feel everything her shadow felt and it was horrible. The creature had managed to wrap itself all around her body and was working to immobilize her arms. She could feel the blood draining from her fingers and she started to get lightheaded and knew there wasn't much time, so she grasped the flashlight with her free hand and twisted her wrists around and struck the creature with the beam. In her head she could hear it hiss and she felt its grip around her lessen enough for her to slip away, but she had only grazed it and it recoiled in front of her ready to strike.

Chance was still looking through her own eyes, but she was ready this time, and when she saw it strike at her shadow she swung the beam down and caught it in mid air sending it to the ether in a swirl of shadowy smoke.

Chance switched off the flashlight, sat

down on the rock slab that she assumed was the couch and willed herself back into the shadow world. Through her shadow's eyes the room became a different place, the walls glowed with the iridescent hue of some indescribable color and the floor was no longer just thousands of small pebbles and rocks, but rather thousands of small pebbles and rocks of every color that wasn't a color she could imagine. The couch she was sitting on was still a rock slab, a very nice looking rock slab, but unfortunately still as uncomfortable as a rock slab. The other furniture in the room was the same, different shades of some unknown color, but still made of rock and stone. There were no pictures on the walls or trinkets on the shelves; this was a place to hide, a small bit of safety in a very unsafe place.

The fox was sitting on a stone block cleaning its paws and looking very much uninterested. "Well that wasn't very pretty."

"No it really wasn't. When I fell I lost my

concentration and couldn't see through my shadow's eyes… everything went wobbly from there. I'm just lucky to be alive. Thanks for getting me the flashlight."

The fox continued to clean its fur.

"So what next?" said Chance.

The fox was scratching its left ear with a hind leg. "Now we get some sleep and wait, hopefully by morning whatever is out there will give up and go looking for food elsewhere. The magic of this place should confuse them enough to forget about us."

Chance was exhausted and sat down on the uncomfortable couch. "Do you think the Hunter has found our trail again?"

"I hope not," said the fox.

"Right," said Chance looking at her scuffed knee, and rubbing her bruises. "Neither do I."

Chance had trouble falling asleep that night, through the rock and stone she couldn't hear the creatures out beyond their hiding spot, but somehow she knew they were there, moving about the rocks and trees looking for them—hungry.

Dusk fell early, and it was dark before he had even reached the forest. Everything around him was dim, but the tracks were clear—the Hunter was back on the trail. He crept along the path, nose to the ground, snuffling and scratching at the dirt. There were two of them now, one on two legs, the other four. The night creatures were stirring and the trees were whispering, but he ignored all of this, they caused him no fear… he was the Hunter, and he was on the hunt.

The fox leaped up on Chance's stomach and pawed at her face. "Wake up now, we need to get moving."

Chance rubbed the sleep from her eyes,

and stretched her aching muscles. This morning she had little difficulty remembering where she was. "I hardly slept last night; rock slabs really don't make for a nice bed."

The fox pushed up against her leg and she scratched him behind the ears. "I slept like a little baby, if that makes you feel any better."

She crept up the stairs and inspected the door to make sure it was closed. There was the tiniest strip of light under the door jam and she knew it must be morning. "No it really doesn't. I swear I could feel them watching us all night."

The fox had followed her up the stairs and stood at the door next to her. "I'm hungry, what else do you have in that bag?"

Chance led him back down the stairs and opened her backpack. She found a half eaten nutty, fruity protein bar wrapped in a foil package which she took a bite from and gave the rest to the fox. "We don't have much food left so make it last."

The fox chewed on the bar without replying.

"Do we have any bright ideas to make it through the day?" said Chance.

"Yes, I think we're going to borrow a boat from a Cyclops."

Twenty minutes later, they had packed up their things and were back on the trail. The coast was clear when they left the cave, but they could see tracks of all shapes and sizes in the mud and grass around the boulders, and more importantly near the entrance to the secret door of the cave, and they knew it was no longer a safe place to be. The forest didn't look any different than it had the day before, but if felt different. It seemed to Chance that it had grown more threatening, as if the trees and shrubs and plants were judging her like it really wasn't a forest at all, but rather someone that didn't like her and most certainly didn't want her lurking about. The trees leaned over the trail, all slanted and at strange intimidating angles watching as she and the fox walked beneath them.

"So borrow a boat from a Cyclops, maybe not such a bad idea," said Chance as she diverted her gaze from the trees and took great interest in her boots.

The fox nodded almost imperceptibly, apparently just as interested in his paws as she was of her boots.

CHAPTER THIRTEEN

One Big Ugly Eye

Less than an hour after they left the cave the trail opened into a field of tree stumps. It was a mass of nettles and weeds, of brambles and thorny snaking vines and prickly bushes that were trying to reclaim the land where the forest was no longer.

The fox had already ducked behind the boulder and was peering into the field. "Quick, get behind these boulders and be quiet… this is where the Cyclops lives. He can't see very well, but he makes up for it with excellent hearing."

Where the field met the river there was a dock, and tied to the dock was a boat, and tied to the boat was a raft that left no question that they had been built from the trees cut from that field. In life, those trees, like the rest of the forest, were frightening with wicked human-like expressions, and twisting branches that reached out at crooked angles so on those dark and stormy nights they could cast terrifying shadows. But now that the dock, the boat, and the raft were constructed from those trees they no longer looked frightening, but rather silly and sad.

The dock was rickety. Much of it was lashed together with cord that had broken and rotted and frayed in so many places that the majority of it was sloping to one side, half submerged in the river with the rest ready to wash away at any moment.

The boat tied to the dock looked worse. More aptly the sinking boat tied to the dock looked worse because much of it had already fallen to pieces, and was probably only floating because the rope, that held it to the dock (that was about to wash away) was keeping it from sinking altogether.

Fortunately, the raft tied up next to the sinking boat looked to be relatively intact, that being only a few of the logs had rotted or come loose, but much of it was still above water. The biggest concern being that it was tied to a sinking boat that was tied to a dock that was about to wash away.

A well beaten trail led from the dock and weaved through the thorny vines and prickly bushes and past the tree stumps to the middle of the field where there was a large weed and grass covered hill with a door in the middle of it, and framed in the opening of that door was a monster.

Howl!

"The Hunter's getting close, I think it's time we discussed your plan about borrowing a boat," whispered Chance.

The fox nodded. "Not much of a plan really, we sneak across the field and borrow that raft, which we'll use to drift down the river… haven't really put much thought to anything after that—honestly didn't think we'd make it this far."

Howl!

"That sounds like an excellent plan to me," whispered Chance. She had already started crawling on her belly toward the field.

She hadn't made it five feet before her foot caught on a thin, nearly invisible thread, and something long and wet and wriggly wrapped around her leg. The next sensation was that of her body being yanked from the ground and thrown into the air. She had triggered a trip wire, she was hanging upside down roughly ten feet off the ground, and being wrenched from the ground and dangling upside down leaves a very unpleasant taste in your mouth.

"Seven, watch out for the trip w…!"

Waaaaah!

"Oh… I see you already found it," said Chance who was now looking into the eyes of the fox as he bobbed up and down next to her hanging from a vine that was wrapped around his tail. "I can see why you didn't much like hanging around like this when I found you… it really isn't very pleasant," she said.

The fox wasn't smiling.

What neither Chance nor the fox knew was that the thin, nearly invisible trip wire, wound its way back to the frame of the front door, and rang a tiny little bell that alerted the Cyclops.

The Cyclops looked out in to the field when the bell rang and grinned. He was hungry which always put him in a foul mood—he hadn't had a bite to eat for nearly a day.

For a Cyclops breaking things is a very normal occurrence, primarily because they have no depth perceptions thanks to the one eye. This in turn makes them live solitary lives in homes with very sturdy furniture. This particular Cyclops was more irritable than the norm, because in addition to not having eaten, he was also tired from not having slept the evening before. Something in the forest was stirring and frightening the night creatures who are not very easily frightened. The trees were also whispering more than usual, and when many whisper it really isn't whispering at all, more like noise, and to a Cyclops with excellent hearing it's very annoying.

At first, Chance thought the Cyclops wasn't much taller than a normal man. And then he moved closer, and he grew until he was standing over them, looking down at them as they hung there nearly ten feet off the ground, which meant that he was at least twelve feet tall. He was ugly, with a single bloodshot eye in the center of his forehead and a stubby horn just above it. His arms were big and burly and muscular, and his body was covered in hair, and scars and scabs, and he smelled like dirt. He was wearing only a tattered loin cloth around his waist and he dragged a gigantic club that was nearly as big as Chance.

"Well don't just hang there, cut us down!" shouted the fox.

Just as Chance was reaching up for her flashlight, the Hunter burst out of the forest and saw all of them there, and it was scarier than Chance had imagined. It looked like a wolf, but much bigger, and with a longer snout which meant more teeth. It was there, but not really there at all. It was flickering between the shadow realm and the solid realm like it didn't belong in either place. For an instant it was black and solid and covered in hair with burning red eyes and mouthful of gleaming white teeth. The next instant it was vapor, mist, a ghost-like apparition that had the shape of a wolf but no tangible body.

It lifted its head to the sky and a puff of steam blew from its nostrils as it began to taste the flavors in the air. Saliva dripped from its lips as it took a step forward in the direction of Chance and the fox testing how far he could push the Cyclops before he attacked.

The Cyclops poked Chance in the stomach, not very hard mind you, just a poke with one of its big, sausage-like fingers. The Hunter flinched and stepped back, anticipating dodging out of the way of the swinging club that never came. The Cyclops didn't even notice the Hunter, and poked Chance again, this time a bit harder.

"Hey… watch it."

The Cyclops flinched, not expecting breakfast to speak, but quickly regained his composure and stepped right back up to her and began sniffing and poking and pulling at her hair which was really unpleasant.

While this was happening, the fox was watching the Hunter slowly approach them with fire burning in his eyes. "Um… I hate to interrupt, but I think someone else is interested in us," said the fox. The Hunter leapt for Chance, all teeth and claws, and she instinctively curled into a little ball which the Cyclops shoved out of the way with his gigantic hand. The teeth and claws of the Hunter missed their mark and found the iron-like forearm of the Cyclops instead. The Cyclops cried in pain and swung his arm back and forth slamming the Hunter into the trees. The Hunter raced forward directly toward the Cyclops, who swung his club at the wrong time, and totally missed the Hunter—but did strike the tree from which Chance and Seven were hanging with such force that it sent them bouncing in the air and knocking the flashlight from her belt where it hit the ground with a *thud*.

"Yeah, I was pretty much hoping that wouldn't happen," said the fox as he bounced up and down and watched the flashlight roll under a log.

Meanwhile the Hunter and the Cyclops were at each other's throats. The Hunter was too fast for the Cyclops, and over and over he would slip between those flailing arms, biting his thighs and legs and arms. The Cyclops would howl in pain, but his thick skin made it difficult to strike a mortal blow.

The Cyclops could only grab tufts of hair, and the occasional lucky glancing punch. Then the Hunter feigned an attack and the Cyclops made a grab for it, and the Hunter rolled out of the way just in time and bit the Cyclops solidly in the hip. That dropped the giant to a knee. The Hunter charged the Cyclops again, and went for the throat to finish him off, but what the Cyclops lacked in speed he made up with brute strength. He swung his club around and with a deafening *crack* caught the Hunter in mid-flight and sent it hurtling backwards.

This time it didn't get back up.

The Cyclops managed to stand, clearly in pain.

"I got the Hunter! I got the Hunter!" the Cyclops gloated. "And now for my prize," and he ripped the vines from the tree and effortlessly tossed Chance and Seven over his should like two fish hanging from a gill line.

"You two will make for good eating… I haven't eaten in days, so hungry I might just eat you raw."

"Raw! Yuck! Don't you know foxes and little girls are much better baked or boiled with fresh vegetables," said Chance. "Anyway, we're nothing but skin and bones; you should fatten us up for a while like a good Christmas goose."

"Yes, she's right of course. You should savor your victory, lock us away for a while and feed us till our bellies are round and our cheeks are plump," said the fox.

"Don't have the energy to fix you up right, very tired, not slept good since the trees started making a racket. Now my leg hurts and I'm more tired and hungry and sore."

They had reached the hill in the middle of the field and the Cyclops pushed the door open. Everything inside was big, giant size, and solid.

Chance expected it to be a mess with bones and rotting carcasses strewn but it was actually neat and clean and a little homey. There was one big room with a little kitchen on one end, stocked with pots and pans and cooking supplies. On the other end of the room was a bed with clean sheets and a big fat teddy bear (with one eye) comfortably resting on a fluffy pillow. In the middle of the room was a sitting area with a comfortable-looking couch, and a big, overstuffed chair. There were drapes on the windows and rugs on the floor… nothing at all like she thought how a Cyclops would live. If she wasn't hanging upside down, ready to be eaten by him, she might actually want to be his friend.

The Cyclops took them to the kitchen and attached the vine to a hook in the ceiling so that they were hanging directly over a huge black cauldron.

Chance was looking at the bed in the

corner of the room. "You must be exhausted after that big fight with the Hunter… your bed sure looks comfortable over there."

The Cyclops was rummaging through a cabinet, but he looked up when she mentioned the bed.

"I think your little bear over there could use some company, maybe you could just take a little nap. When you wake up we'll still be here, and you can cook us up right and make a fine meal with vegetables, and stuffing, and maybe a sweet fruity dessert. It would sure be a waste to eat us now when you can savor us later."

"But I'm hungry now."

Chance smiled. "I'll tell you what, I have some snacks in my bag that you can have, and then you can eat us later. We really don't have any need for them anyway. …I promise they taste great."

The Cyclops sniffed her bag and thought about her proposal for a moment. "No tricks…

or I'll just eat you now."

"No tricks… just snacks," said Chance.

The Cyclops lifted her from the hook and set her on the ground. Chance slipped the bag from her shoulders, and searched around until she found all of the energy bars she had left. She pulled the wrapper from a big, thick chocolaty bar that probably had enough calories to keep her going for the rest of the day and handed it to the Cyclops.

The Cyclops ran his nose over the bar and scratched at it with his finger before sampling a small bite. Chance held her breath, hoping that he would like it, but she needn't worry a second later the bar was gone and there was a huge smile on his face.

"Told you so… I knew you'd like it."

The Cyclops grinned and pushed a vanilla flavored bar into his mouth in one bite, aware that Chance was looking at the door.

"Oh no you don't little girly. These are

great snacks, but I'm still eating you and the fox later," said the Cyclops as he effortlessly lifted her from the ground and hooked the vine to the ceiling.

Satisfied for the moment the Cyclops hobbled over to the bed and snuggled up to his stuffed bear.

They waited for him to fall asleep, but they didn't have to wait long before his snoring became so loud it reverberated off the walls and shook the sturdy furniture.

The fox made a snuffling noise. "So that's great you bought a little time… what's up your sleeve?" he whispered.

Chance smiled and lifted her sleeve. There, shoved under her watchband, was a small penlight on a keychain concealed nicely by her jacket. She pulled the flashlight out from under her watch and stuck it in her mouth so she could use both hands to pull herself up and grab onto the vine above her leg. Holding on with one hand she switched on the light and cut through the vine with the dagger-like beam of light and oh so quietly dropped to the ground before cutting the vine for the fox.

They crept to the door and quietly pushed it open. Unfortunately they didn't know about the tiny bell that rang as the door opened. The Cyclops was on his feet faster than they thought was possible.

"Run," yelled Chance. "I'm going to get the flashlight, you get to the raft!"

The fox didn't argue and raced to the dock.

The Cyclops threw the door open and took off after the girl. He tripped over the first tree stump he came across; falling on his face with such force Chance felt the ground shake. He was up quickly, though, and back on her tail. He might be clumsy, but he was fast, mostly because he was twelve feet tall with long legs.

Chance was struggling through the weeds

and vines and brambles and if it wasn't for the Cyclops' bad leg, he probably would have caught up with her. Finally she reached the spot where they had been trapped and searched for the light, finding it under the log where it had fallen, but the Cyclops was already on her, and she grabbed it just in time. She stumbled backwards over a log and fell, landing hard on a large flat rock. The Cyclops saw his opportunity and moved toward her, swinging his fist to pummel her, but she rolled out of the way and his fist slammed into the rock breaking his knuckles.

The Cyclops howled in pain. Chance leaped to her feet and raced into the forest. Maybe he wouldn't be able to get through. But he was right behind her, tearing through the underbrush. Chance turned back the way she had come—back into the field of stumps and weeds and brambles. She ran as fast as her legs would carry her, not turning until she reached the dock and leaped onto the sinking boat and then onto the raft.

The fox was trying to untie the knot in the rope that tied the raft to the dock, but knots and such things can be tricky when you don't have any thumbs. Chance turned when she saw the fox's eyes bulge. The Cyclops was leaping onto the boat, but when he landed, his weight was too much for the rotting vessel and he crashed through the deck. He was struggling through the water swinging his fists at the hull trying to get to the raft, but Chance already had switched on her flashlight and sliced through the rope freeing the raft from the dock and allowing the river's current to take them away.

CHAPTER FOURTEEN
Wild Ride

Chance fell backwards, panting. "That wasn't fun at all."

The fox eased up next to her. "Thanks, I wasn't much in the mood to be boiled."

Chance rolled her head over to look at him. "Was that a compliment?"

The fox grinned. "Take it anyway you like."

"You know, when I went to find the flashlight, the Hunter wasn't there," said Chance.

If the fox blinked Chance didn't even notice. "I didn't think we would have gotten rid of him so easily... he's probably off licking his wounds and thinking about what he's going to do when he finds us again. I seriously doubt that will be the last we see of him."

Chance rolled her head back and looked

up at the sky and sighed. Neither one of them spoke as they drifted with the current for the rest of the afternoon, past the oppression of the trees that didn't want them there, and past the predators and prey alike who peered at them from the darkness between the trunks with hunger and malice in their eyes, and long sinister grins on their faces.

There was a wooden tiller attached to the back of the raft that Chance used to try and steer them, but the current was swift, and the rough wood left splinters in her palms. The swift current meant that they were quickly passing through the forest, and moving too fast for anything to catch up with them on land, or for that matter, reach up from under the dark river waters with long, wriggly tentacles. The down side, and she only realized this when she remembered what the fox had said about the castle, was that she had no idea how to slow down, and somewhere at the end of the river was a waterfall that cascaded into the great bottomless abyss.

The fox was the first to break the silence. "It won't be long before the Hunter informs the Shadow King that you exist."

"So… how's that worse than the situation we are already in?"

The fox scratched behind its ears and rubbed its paws on its whiskers in a way that managed to show impatience. "Well the only way into or out of this place is with the *book*, and seeing as though he has the book, I'll bet he will put two and two together and figure you have some pages from that book."

"Ah… I see what you mean. That isn't very good news, is it?"

The fox didn't answer.

"So what's next?" asked Chance.

"We still have to figure out a way to sneak into the castle and get to the portal without being caught. This will be a bit more difficult now that the Shadow King knows that you're out here. By the end of the day, he'll have half of his army looking for us. The Hunter will have told him you are traveling with a fox, and because he knows foxes have superior intellects, he already knows that I know something about this place, and that I will have told you the only way out is through the castle."

"Oh...."

"Yes, 'Oh' indeed," said the fox.

"Superior intellect huh."

"Yes," said the fox.

The river began to narrow, and the raft began moving faster. They had left the forest behind and were drifting into a canyon with high rock walls overgrown and tangled with vines, and tenacious trees, and scrub that clung to the rock. For a short time it was a beautiful sight to see. The canyon was layer upon layer of colors that she had no words to describe, and the trees and vines that clung so desperately to those walls were full of life, and flowers, and happiness.

Gradually the canyon began to narrow, becoming ever tighter and tighter and the shadows grew deeper and the light began to dim. The walls had become sheer, washed smooth from the river, and the tangled overgrowth thinned until it finally disappeared leaving the rock bare and lifeless.

The raft was moving faster and the water began churning and rolling, and the further in they traveled, the faster the river ran and the rougher it became. The water was no longer dark and calm, but a color that wasn't white, crashing against the walls, pitching the raft from side to side, and spraying high into the air, soaking them both.

Chance was scared. She tried to steer the vessel, but when she grabbed the tiller, the raft listed sideways and was sucked into a whirlpool behind a boulder, spinning out of control, ripping the tiller from her hand. She tried to grab it again, but the raging water was swinging it back and forth so fast she couldn't get it.

They were stuck behind the boulder. Chance knew something had to be done, so she threw her whole body at the tiller. The tiller struck her in the gut and knocked her off her feet, but somehow she managed to hold on and regain her footing. She heaved as hard as she could until the tiller moved where she wanted it to go. Chance was able to steer the boat around the boulder and into the raging river. The water was tumbling and twisting, racing over rocks and through narrow channels, over and down small waterfalls and chutes that were driving them ever faster towards the abyss.

Chance grabbed the fox, slung him into her jacket, and crawled to the middle of the raft. There she could do nothing more than clutch onto one of the logs and hang on for dear life as the raft banged and smashed off rocks and into the walls, and started tearing apart around them.

Within minutes there was nothing left. All the ropes and vines that had tied and held the logs together had snapped. The raft disintegrated, breaking apart; leaving them stranded and perilously clinging to only one log.

They heard the great waterfall before they saw it. It was roaring in the distance, the sound of millions of gallons of water rushing over rocks and boulders and through narrow channels, compressing into an unstoppable force until, suddenly, it must fall away over the edge of the void and dissipate into a cloud of mist.

All Chance could do was hang on. There was no steering or stopping the log. It was nothing more than a twig in a typhoon being dragged along with the flow, and they were nothing more than tiny ants clinging on desperately to that twig, hoping these were not the last seconds of their lives. They bounced from one rock to the next, side to side, from one wall of the canyon to the other.

Strangely enough, the closer they came to the edge of the abyss the quieter it became. The rage and the roar was lessening and the sound became hollow. It was not the intense bellow or boom that she expected would be near the edge, but more solemn like even the water knew it had nowhere to go. There was no bottom to these falls, no place where the water could strike the earth with a boom and rumble before it raged onward towards another river or lake or even an ocean where it would slow and become part of a greater body of water and complete the cycle. No, this water would disappear into a bottomless void and leave this place, wasted and unused.

There was no stopping the log before it fell over the edge. Chance clung on to the fox, not willing to let him go, and squeezed shut her eyes just as she felt the world disappear beneath her and they fell into the darkness without a sound.

CHAPTER FIFTEEN

Six Legs Are Better Than Seven

Fortunately, the fall only lasted a couple of seconds before it was over.

Cautiously she opened her eyes, hoping she would see puffy white clouds, and beautiful castles, and angels, harps, and happiness. She desperately hoped it wouldn't be fire and brimstone, and lost souls paying the price for their sins, and evil ways.

When she did open her eyes, it wasn't either one. She was still holding the fox, and she was still alive, and still wet… and now stuck. She was stuck in an enormous spider's web that spanned between one of the giant mushroom-like trees and a rock outcropping that jutted out from behind the waterfall about twenty feet under the rim.

She squeezed the fox, and cried and

wriggled and jiggled and thoroughly enjoyed begin alive. "We're alive fox... we're alive."

The fox smiled and licked her nose. "Yes we are."

Chance continued to wriggle and jiggle and be happy.

"Chance, Chance," the fox perked an ear, "Chance stop moving... please stop wriggling around."

"Why, why would I want to stop, we're alive. That river is huge, just look at it. What are the chances of us falling into a spider web, I mean it's a big web, but still."

"I don't know, *Chance*. What are the chances of such a thing happening?"

Chance smiled.

"Now stop wriggling," said the fox.

"Why?"

"Do I really need to explain to you why it's not a good idea to wriggle and jiggle and thrash about in a spider's web?"

Chance stopped bouncing about and looked over at the mushroom-like tree, or more precisely at what was climbing out from under the canopy of the mushroom-like tree. "No, I suppose you don't."

The fox was watching it. "From the frying pan and into the fire."

"Said the spider to the fly," whispered Chance.

"All right, I have a plan," said the fox.

"*You* have a plan?"

"That's not what I meant. I meant that…" said Chance, but she was interrupted by a buzz in the web, and when she turned to see the source she saw that the spider had taken interest in their presence.

"Now do you want to hear my plan?" asked Seven.

"Yes, yes let's hear what you've got."

"All right, this is what we're going to do. You give me that little penlight of yours and hide me in your coat. When the spider comes over here, it will wrap you up in a web sac and carry you to its lair to soften up. You'll have to stew for a while because spiders need their food liquefied before they can eat it... something about their anatomy that prevents them from eating solid food—but I digress. Once it leaves you to liquefy, I'll cut us out and we can be on our merry way."

"This is your plan? Your plan involves me getting me all wrapped up like a mummy and dragged off to liquefy so that I can presumably be eaten, or I suppose drank, at some point in the foreseeable future," said Chance.

"Yes, that's it."

"Well how do you know it won't just kill me on the spot then wrap me up?"

The fox didn't take his eyes off the spider that was quickly approaching, but something wasn't quite right. It was huge, easily ten feet tall and eighteen feet across, but it wasn't a spider at all. It had the body of a jungle cat, but with six legs instead of four, and eight fierce eyes that were arranged vertically, four on each side of the feline-like head each full of hunger, purpose, and delight over what must be a fine catch. The creature crept closer, hissing with each step, and with every breath it took venom dripped from its fangs searing the web in the places it touched.

Sizzle, buzz.

Closer it crept, more terrible with every step, and every hunger filled gaze it cast upon them.

The fox dug deeper into the folds of Chance's jacket. "That's no spider, it's a nightwalker. The good news is that it won't kill you because it likes fresh meat, not dead and cold… just soft."

Chance didn't reply… the nightwalker was already there.

Chance cowered into the web and curled herself into a little ball. The creature towered over her and poked at her with one of its legs and Chance lurched back, entangling deeper into the web.

With its cluster of eyes, the nightwalker examined the catch, poking and prodding at it, pleased ever time it twisted and squirmed… he loved his quarry fresh and warm and feisty. He was hungry, but he knew his feasting would have to wait until he was safe in his den. The creature lifted his tail and whipped it over his shoulder so that the tip of it struck the girl in the arm. He didn't want her dead, just quiet until he was ready for a meal.

Chance felt a sudden stinging pain in her arm and she realized that the creature had a stinger on its tail—and she'd just been stung. Her fingers started to tingle and then her arm started to feel numb and soon the numbness spread all over her body and the sky wasn't so bright anymore and a moment later everything went black.

The creature waited until his catch stopped moving, then with his powerful jaws he picked her up by her jacket and carried her back to his den where he would hang her and let her stew.

His current home was a series of tunnels, cracks, and holes that dug into the granite walls of the chasm. For miles they stretched into the earth, snaking their way through the stone and dirt beneath the river and forest and deep within the trees of the whispering woods. They reeked of death and decay, but sometimes the forest could be worse, and he used that to his advantage. For many a creature wandered into these holes in hopes of finding passage under the forest, but few ever returned—most only found him.

Chance woke a few minutes later, but she still couldn't move, the toxin had paralyzed her from head to toe. Only once before had Chance encountered a darkness this deep, and she still didn't like it. The tunnel stretched on forever, and after a while even the sound of the falls dissipated to that of only a rumble somewhere in the distance. Far too soon even that had silenced and the only sounds she could hear was the labored breathing of the creature and the occasional *plink* of water dripping into some invisible basin.

To say that Chance was scared was an understatement, but she held herself together. There was still some hope that the fox's plan might work.

After what seemed like hours, a dim light flickered ahead of them, growing brighter as they approached. Eventually they came upon the entrance to a vast chamber with a sunken floor and Chance could hear what sounded like running water. There was light in the great room, radiating from some type of incandescent fungus that grew on the walls, and if she was in different circumstances would probably have been beautiful because it was a wealth of unnamable colors in hues and shades that shouldn't be possible. She could see massive columns of rock spanning from ceiling to floor with great webs stretching between them ready to ensnare any fool that came too close, and she assumed that this creature must have done away with the spider that had created these webs and the one under waterfall, because she doubted it could spin a web of its own.

The nightwalker lifted the girl to an outcropping of rock and with the aid of its tail entangled a well used web line around her ankles leaving her about five feet off the ground. Beneath her was a pile of bones and clothes and weapons and revolting things that Chance did not wish to look at and certainly not smell.

Looking pleased with his catch, the creature gave the girl a poke in the ribs that caused her to swing back and forth and make her feel dizzy and sick. The creature lifted its head and extended his jaws allowing two huge fangs to extend from his mouth, each dripping with some kind of venom that sizzled as it fell to the floor. Chance tried to wiggle and squirm, but she still couldn't move her body, all she could do was watch as the nightwalker titled its head back ready to take a bite out of her.

Suddenly the room began to buzz as all of the webs started resonating, humming like a guitar that was slightly out of tune. The creature looked away from Chance and reached its tail up, touching a strand of web just over his head. The web must have told him something because it raced across the room to a tunnel that led away from the chamber in the opposite direction they had come from. He glanced back to the girl, as if in indecision, but apparently the call of the web was more appealing than a meal that surely wasn't about to go anywhere, and he disappeared into the tunnel leaving the girl alone in the semi-darkness.

Chance waited as patiently as anyone could wait while hanging upside down, still paralyzed, and just having just been nearly eaten, as she imagined anyone could patiently wait.

"All right, he's gone… get me out of here."

Chance could feel the fox squirming around then he poked his head out from under her jacket.

"Now where's that 'on' button?"

The switch clicked on and a razor thin beam of light blazed from the lens. "Ah got it."

With the penlight in the fox's mouth he sliced through the web line freeing Chance's ankles and she dropped onto the pile of bones and rolled to the floor. "I have to say I am really, really tired of hanging upside down."

The fox didn't reply, but had a smug look on his face.

"I would wipe that look of your face.

You were all wrapped up in my jacket, but I was a heartbeat away from becoming dinner. If some poor other creature didn't get caught in the web I would have surely been eaten right then and there." She poked the fox in the head. "And by *I*, I mean *we*."

"Yes, but you weren't," said the fox. "And it looks like the toxin is wearing off."

"No I suppose I wasn't, but it was still a bad plan, and yes I can feel my arms and legs now," said Chance.

"So what was that thing, I don't think it had anything to do with making these webs."

"No the nightwalkers are nothing but thieves, they take what they want and settle were they please. One of them took up residence at the castle while I was still there, and it took forever to get rid of it. I suppose when these webs rot away and are no longer useful it will abandon this place and find new hunting grounds," said the fox.

The fox hopped up on the skull of what could only have been from a small dragon and began cleaning the webbing from his fur. "If you're about finished, I think now would be a good time to find a way out."

Chance slipped the penlight into her pocket and removed the flashlight from her belt.

Chance pointed in the direction that the nightwalker went. "It went that way, so I'm thinking we go that way," as she pointed in the opposite direction, "back in the direction we came. I'm pretty sure I saw a bunch of tunnels that branched off from this one. Hopefully one of them will get us out of here."

Chance lifted herself up on wobbly legs and took a couple of slow steps forward, a bit unsteady and not nearly ready to run, but well enough to travel.

They walked and searched and walked some more. The rock was dark, and slick, and smooth to the touch, and when Chance cast her beam on the walls a million, million crystals glistened like the night sky which would have been very cool if she and the fox hadn't been wandering for the last hour completely lost.

"Don't foxes have some kind of sixth sense about finding their way home?" said Chance.

Seven looked up at the girl. "We're foxes, not homing pigeons, I'm afraid we don't have any special 'find our way out of cave tunnel senses.'" The fox stopped. "*Shhh*, I think I hear something."

"I don't hear anything, what do you hear?"

"Hush, I'm a fox. That means I can hear much better than you, so *shhh* and let me listen. It sounds like we're on the right track; I think I can hear running water. Hopefully this tunnel will lead us out of here."

"Good. I can't stand being under all of this rock, and I really think I'm getting claustrophobic," said Chance.

"Let's see, you were just captured by a giant eight eyed, six legged panther, paralyzed, and carried off into its den to become an evening meal. I doubt it's claustrophobia that's got you agitated."

Chance used her thumb and fore finger to create a little gun and pointed at the fox. "*Touché.*"

They continued down the tunnel in silence, listening for any sound that the river might be ahead of them. She hoped it wasn't her imagination, but it did sound like it was getting louder. Then in the distance, Chance could see a faint dot of light far ahead. Not long after, and to their great relief, the light grew brighter and the sound of the river became louder and louder, until it was almost deafening. Finally they could see the end of the tunnel and thought they just might make it out of this maze once and for all well, but that hope didn't last too long.

The nightwalker had found them. He approached on the ceiling, drifting silently and invisibly through the darkness, and only a loose stone that was jarred free by a misstep warned them.

Chance and the fox saw him there, all eyes and legs and venom. They raced to the light, to the end of the passageway, and to freedom. They emerged from the tunnel onto an amazing scene. They stood at the edge of the waterfall, close enough for Chance to run her finger across the wall of water as it cascaded down and fell away into oblivion. In front of them spanned the vast emptiness of the pit, dark and sinister, nothing but mist and mystery. In the distance they could see the Shadow King's castle floating impossibly above the bottomless hole, the only access being a long and twisting bridge made from stone and steel. Guarding access to the bridge was an enormous creature with the body of dragon and three heads, one of a lion, one of an eagle, and one of a bear.

The three-headed fiend was the least of their problems. The tunnel they'd emerged from was more than a hundred feet below the rim of the pit, with nothing but a sheer wall of rock above and all around them. There was no escape. The wall was impossible to climb. Directly behind them waited the nightwalker… far too patiently.

The nightwalker knew he had been spotted, leapt down from the ceiling, and slowly made his way to the end of the tunnel. He could hear the blood pumping through the little girl and the fox, and sensed their fear. There was no need to hurry. For many of years now, he had been the King of these tunnels and he knew where each of them led. But the girl had proved to be elusive, it wasn't often that his prey escaped his clutches and he didn't want to take any chances… this time his stinger would be venomous.

The creature slowly moved toward them

on six powerful legs and Chance knew there was nothing left to do but fight. She pulled her flashlight from her belt and clicked it on releasing the brilliant beam of light that grew into a blazing sword. "Get back, you big ugly beast, or I'll stick you," Chance said.

But the nightwalker had been in many fights in his long years. His hide was thick and strong, and no man or beast had bested him in battle. He cared little of idle threats, especially from those of a little girl. So he advanced on the girl, swift and dangerous racing towards her with his stinger ready to strike. But Chance did the unexpected and dived forward between the creature's legs. Chance saw her opportunity and rolled onto her back while swinging the blade in an arc over her head striking the creature's tail as it swept past her and cleanly sliced off the stinger.

The nightwalker had never felt such pain before and he lurched back and away from the girl, shrieking in agony. The wound oozed blood and poison leaving a smoldering trail on the ground and he crept back into the tunnel and to the comfortable darkness.

A horrible idea occurred to Chance. "Hey you big ugly beast, get back here and fight me. What… you gonna let a little girl beat you? You might look like a panther, but you're nothing but a chicken. *Buk, buk, buk, buk, buk!*"

"Chance, whoa, that's probably not such a good idea," said the fox that had already backed away about as far as he could without falling into the pit.

Chance ignored him.

The creature forgot about his misery. He wasn't about to get bested by a puny little human. He was the King of these tunnels, dangerous and feared and most of all hungry. This was not the end of the battle, and even though the little girl had a stinger of her own, he wasn't about to run away from a perfectly good meal. The nightwalker charged from the darkness straight toward Chance all fangs and legs and anger, but again Chance was ready and once more she did the unexpected.

Chance had moved herself just behind a boulder and when she knew that the creature had taken the bait she leaped onto the big rock and waited for just the right moment. That moment happened fast and just as the monster came at her she leapt off the boulder and onto the creature's back, wrapping her legs around his neck. The nightwalker thrashed and bucked, but Chance held on as tight as she could, because if she fell she was doomed.

"Listen to me nightwalker, if you don't stop thrashing about, I'm going to stick you," yelled Chance.

The creature flailed and shook and smashed into the tunnel walls, but Chance never let go.

"Stop now," yelled Chance as she swung

the beam of the flashlight over the nightwalker's head, searing off a thin layer of skin and fur. That enraged the beast, but it did get his attention and he stopped knocking about.

"Little fool, I will drive my fangs into you and turn you to gel so I can eat you from the inside out," said the nightwalker.

"Eeuw, that's just nasty—and I knew you could speak." said Chance.

"Your voice is like needles in my head. Stop blathering and get down here so I can eat you," said the beast.

"I'm not about to get down until you hear me out. I have a proposition for you."

"What kind of absurd proposition could a miserable little urchin like you have to offer me?"

Chance smiled and leveled the beam from the flashlight just far enough over the nightwalker's head for him to feel the heat radiating from the blade and remind him that she wasn't fooling around. "I suppose the kind of proposition that prevents either one of us from dying."

The creature flinched away from the searing heat of the blade. "All right, you have my attention, I'm listening. The nightwalker moved to the center of the tunnel and remained still. "Speak little fool, before I change my mind."

"Right, the fox and I need to get to the Shadow King's castle, and we need to do it without anyone knowing."

The creature made a squealing, hissing, cackling noise that made Chance cringe. It was like fingernails on a chalk board, and for a moment Chance thought it was some kind of attack. Then she realized that the nightwalker was trying to laugh. "You are a fool... why would you want to go there? There's nothing but trolls and ogres, and a slow death for you there. With me at least you can die quickly and painlessly."

The nightwalker hissed. "So how exactly does this *proposition* help me?"

Chance dipped the beam of the flashlight down close to the creature's head singeing his fur. "I suppose I won't have to poke you with my stick."

The nightwalker cringed, but didn't speak.

"Look, I'm hungry, tired and cranky, so please just listen. If I repeat myself, I might just change my mind. We want to go to the Shadow King's castle and not be seen and there's no way we could get across that bridge without being caught. I'm thinking you could carry us on your back while you climb across the underside of the bridge and no one will ever know we're down there. I mean who would be crazy enough to ride upside-down on the back of a nightwalker on the bottom side of a bridge over a bottomless pit to a floating castle where nothing but death awaits us?"

"So, how do I know that if I help you, you won't just try to kill me?" said the nightwalker.

"Because if I wanted to kill you, I would have already done so, and at any rate if I did I wouldn't be able to cross the bridge."

This made some sense to the creature. "What about when we get close to the other side, what if you try to stick me then?" asked the nightwalker.

"Because if I stick you before we reach the castle we would all fall to our deaths and that would make no sense at all."

So the nightwalker agreed to carry the girl and the fox on his back across the bridge.

"Seven, come on. We've got our ride to the castle," yelled Chance.

The fox simply sauntered across the tunnel, between the nightwalker's two front legs and under the creature's belly before leaping up on to the boulder and into Chances waiting arms.

The nightwalker walked to the edge of the tunnel and looked out into the abyss. "Last chance, little girl. If you let me eat you now, I promise I'll be quick about it... you won't even feel a thing. I doubt the Shadow King will offer you such a good deal."

"Thank you very much, but we'll take our chances my way."

"Suit yourself."

The nightwalker crawled down the sheer wall of the pit on dagger-like claws that cut through the rock like butter, disappearing into the swirling mist and fog, and out of sight of anyone or anything that might be watching from the bridge. A few minutes later he emerged from the fog and climbed the wall directly under the bridge until he had reached the underside of the stone structure, then he began his upside-down trek to the castle. It was a very unnerving trip. Chance had used a line of cord she had in her pack, and tied it around the nightwalker to keep her from falling into the darkness, but she still wrapped her legs around the creature with all her might, and clung to the line of rope, and refused to open her eyes.

It was not easy walking; the underside bridge to the castle was rugged and dangerous even for the nightwalker that could walk on almost anything. The stone was uneven and jagged, forcing the creature to precariously step from one outcropping and overhang to the next, slipping on more than one occasion, and lurching from side to side quite a bit, and generally making Chance very nervous.

At last the nightwalker crawled out from under the bridge and down the castle's walls until he was underneath the castle and out of site of the patrols on the bridge, sentries on the ramparts, and guards walking the parapets. The nightwalker crossed under the foundation of the castle until he reached the opposite side of the castle. There, he scaled back up the wall until he found a suitable place to let them off.

He had found a drainage pipe which was easily large enough for Chance to stand up in, and stopped on a ledge just below it. "So I've done what you asked. You'd might as well go ahead and get it over with."

Chance opened her eyes and began to untie herself from the creature's back. "Get what over with?"

"I have no stinger and I cannot reach around far enough to bite you with my fangs, and even if I could I'm sure you would be able to stick me just as quickly and kill us both," groaned the nightwalker.

Chance leapt off the nightwalker and coiled the rope back into her pack. She unzipped her jacket and scratched the fox's ears. "We're there you can come out now."

Seven leapt from the folds of Chance's jacket and landed on a ledge just below the drain pipe, not taking his eyes off the beast.

Chance lifted the fox up into the drain pipe which was wet and slippery and smelled bad. She then pulled herself up into the pipe turning her back to the creature. "Because, nightwalker, that is not the kind of person I am. Now please go back to the tunnels you live in and remember what happened this day."

The nightwalker hesitated for a moment, and then he turned and walked back down the wall and disappeared into the mist.

CHAPTER SIXTEEN

The Castle

Chance was utterly and totally miserable. There were many things in this place between night and day that Chance could not understand, or dream of, but smell was not one of those things. She hadn't really thought much about it until now. The forest they had traveled through smelled green and moldy and damp, just like a forest should, and the cave and tunnels smelled old and musty, and the river smelled wet and maybe a bit fishy. But the smell of this tunnel was not one of those things. It smelled disgusting, and gross, and nasty, and foul, and of many more things that she would like to never smell again.

From the minute they had entered the tunnel the fox had taken refuge in her arms which seemed to have become a comfortable place for him.

They were walking against the flow of a slow-moving, shin-deep, river of water that was unmistakably sewage. There were clumps and globs of filth and debris and refuse bumping against her legs and catching on her boots, and when she hit one just right it would release a new and unimaginable stench that made her stomach tremble and shudder and twist. The pipe was dark and moldy with slick walls covered in slime and fungus and goo that dangled from the roof and stuck to her hands when she touched it, and into her hair, and on her face when she had to push through it in those places that it clogged the pipe.

Along the way they passed by a number of ladders that exited the tunnel, but all of the ones they tried led to a dead end or an occupied room.

Then finally they came to a ladder that led up through the ceiling of the pipe and Chance climbed up it, holding tight to the rungs because they were slippery and slimy. The ladder led them into a room that must have once been a kitchen, and they were climbing up the rubbish chute. The room was old and moldy, and smelled stale as though it hadn't been used in ages. But by now, Chance couldn't be totally sure about that because her nose wasn't working so well.

Chance peered out through a metal grate that separated the chute from the room. There wasn't too much to the room. It wasn't very large, and all that it contained was an old log-burning stove, and a sturdy looking wooden table with tarnished pots and pans hanging above it, and a wash basin with rusted pipes and moldy dishes stacked high, and other assorted kitchen goods, but all of it looked tired and old and no longer usable.

The fox nodded. "Open the grate and let me explore for a bit and I'll come right back."

Chance nodded and pushed open the

grate which squeaked on rusty hinges and made her cringe. "Go on, see what you can find, I'll wait here for you."

The fox took off across the room and Chance dropped back down the ladder and waited for him to return. She decided to wait for the fox in case this place wasn't safe.

Chance waited, and after about fifteen minutes of waiting, he hadn't returned. She started to worry. After nearly a half hour had passed, he still hadn't returned. She was halfway up the ladder to go look for him when he strutted back into the room.

Chance climbed the rest of the way up the ladder and pulled the fox into her arms. "Where have you been? You nearly scared me to death. I thought maybe you had been captured, or worse… especially after you telling me just how tasty a treat foxes can be. I was about to go looking for you."

The fox jumped out of her arms and onto

a narrow ledge out of the rubbish bin. "Coming to find me wouldn't have been such a good idea, and with a stench like that you'd be caught for sure."

"So where are we?"

"We're in a section of the castle at the base of one of the spires, near one of the castle's outer walls. We're not too far from the portal room. I didn't run into anyone until I was very close to the portal, so I think we're in an unused section of the castle. It should be safe for you to get out of the sewer drain."

Chance climbed out of the drain and dumped her backpack on the ground. She fished around through the pack and pulled out a clean t-shirt as well as a bottle of anti-bacterial gel. "OK… how about you go keep lookout while I try to get some of this stench off."

The fox sniffed and turned up his nose at her and traipsed back into the hall. "Good idea," he said under his breath.

Chance changed her shirt and wiped herself down as best she could until she thought most of the stench was gone. Then, as she was stuffing her dirty clothes back into her pack, a small flashlight rolled out from one of the side pockets. She picked it up and turned it round in her hand, *forgot I had this*, she said to herself, and without thinking jammed it down inside her boot instead of back in the pack. A few minutes later and considerably cleaner she stuck her head out the door and called the fox back in.

The fox circled around her and sniffed her legs. "Yes, a bit better. Now maybe that stink won't give us away."

"Good. I was seriously starting to offend myself."

"We need to find the portal room, and do it without being seen," said the fox.

Chance looked out of the kitchen, up and down the halls, but it wasn't at all what she imagined a castle should look like. Of course she had never been in a castle before, but she didn't imagine it would look like this. She pictured gilded walls and beautiful paintings and marble columns, but the halls were dark and gloomy and smelled of dust and mold and decay and she didn't like it at all.

She stepped into the hall, and suddenly felt disoriented and dizzy. The walls started to blur and shift and everything felt like it was swaying and tilting. So she stepped back into the kitchen and the swaying stopped and everything went solid again.

The fox followed her back in. "Right, I forgot to mention that this place isn't really here, but sort of everywhere at the same time, I imagine it's a bit disorienting if you aren't used to it."

Chance rested her hand on the sturdy table, and just looked at the fox. "What are you talking about?"

"This place, I don't just mean this castle,

but this whole world exists at the instant between night and day. This exact moment in time, countless eons ago, was the moment that the darkness was banished from the universe. You see, before time existed, the universe was controlled by darkness... the total absence of light. Then in a flash that all changed and the darkness was given a name and banished from the universe and sent to this place. Suns and stars were born creating galaxies made from a billion, billion stars, and lit up the universe casting their glowing rays of light across the cosmos. But light without darkness is hardly better than total darkness. Thus the darkness was allowed to return, and when that happened the universe began to take shape, but the darkness could only return as a shadow, and that it could be driven away by the light. But in the caves and under the rocks and in all the lightless places of the worlds the darkness grew weary and angry, and no longer wished to be governed by the light. In arrogance and pride, it took on the name of the Shadow King and expanded and covered the worlds in thick layers of clouds too dense for the light to penetrate.

The Shadow King's crimes could not be tolerated, and once man was strong enough he created the book, and the portal, and banished him to this place until he would be set free."

"But there is still darkness at night, and under beds, and in closets, and pretty much anywhere the lights are turned off," said Chance while looking around. "Well at least in my world that is."

The fox cleaned one of his front paws. "Exactly, darkness still exists… it has to in order to keep the balance, but it has no real power. The creatures that once came from shadow, monsters, and ogres, and ghouls, and fiends, and all the other creatures of fae… the things that go bump in the night have been banished here, and only here in this place that exists at the moment between night and day do they have power. In your world, all you have to do is turn on the lights and the shadows are forced back to this place."

Chance understood. "Light drives the darkness away, and while the Shadow King and his minions are imprisoned in this place, they have no real power in my world," she squeezed the handle of the flashlight, "or from the light that comes from my world."

The fox grinned showing too many teeth. "I forgot to mention that the flashlight is only a flashlight in this castle. It will guide you through the darkness, but it won't be able to harm anything unless, of course, you use it to smack someone over the head."

Chance slumped. "Why?"

"Because this castle really isn't here… or at least not really, it exists totally out of time and space. It has to be like that to keep the Shadow King trapped. Outside of this castle, the world is solid and the shadows can be chased away, but this castle is the Shadow King's home and his last refuge. In this place he still retains his power; the light will not drive him away."

"Can he leave the castle, and go into the forests, and see the countryside and visit the mountains?" asked Chance.

The fox hesitated for a moment like he was thinking. "Yes, but some part of him is always trapped here, so he can leave, but not totally."

"I guess I understand," said Chance, not really understanding but found no real reason to mention that to the fox.

"You'll probably need to see through your own eyes again to find your way through the castle. Too much of this place exists completely in shadow; it will just make you sick and confused. Just stay close to me and I'll get us where we need to go," said Seven.

Chance closed her eyes and relaxed, and

thought of what her world looked like and how she looked in that world, and what red and green and blue looked like, and everything she could think of that reminded her of home. When she opened her eyes the castle was a different place. The kitchen was still a kitchen and it still looked old and unused, but everything looked a bit different. Not physically different, just different. The shadows and shading of everything were reversed. The dark places were now white instead of black. A table looked like a table and a chair like a chair, but they cast white shadows and not dark ones. It was very bizarre, but at least it didn't make her feel sick.

Chance pushed off the table and walked back to the hall. "OK, I'm not looking through my shadow's eyes. Now all the light and dark places are reversed, and it looks strange, but doesn't make me feel weird. I'm going to try the hall again."

The fox licked his front paws.

Chance closed her eyes and stepped into the hall. She steadied herself against the doorframe and hoped it wouldn't make her woozy again. Slowly she opened her eyes and the hall didn't make her dizzy or wobbly; now it was just gloomy and moldy, and strange, and reversed.

Chance followed behind the fox without speaking. He seemed to know where he was going and she wasn't about to argue.

But they hadn't been out of the kitchen for ten minutes when the fox stopped them, and ducked behind a corner just in time to avoid being seen by two creatures. They were short and brownish-green, with thick, scaly skin, and filthy black hair. They had fat round faces with long noses and dirty grey eyes. Their mouths were long and too big for their faces with twisted yellow teeth poking out from under their lips in all the wrong directions.

"The master will return soon. He said to

keep out of his way, and stay out of sight. I think he's planning something."

"I don't like it when he plans things… one of us always gets dead," said the other.

"I know," said the first.

Chance and the fox crept back down the hall in the direction they'd come from, and hid in the recess of a door.

They waited for a few minutes and cautiously crept back down the hall and peered around the corner, but the ogres had left. They followed the hall for another few minutes, slowing at every corner they came to, but they didn't run into anyone else. The fox seemed to know where he was going and hardly hesitated even when they came to intersections or stairs or doors that they had to pass through, which made Chance very nervous when she had to open them. The further they got, the faster he moved, but Chance figured he was just as anxious to get out this place as she was… probably even more so she thought.

The fox then stopped at the top of a narrow flight of stairs that led down into the darkness. He looked up at the girl and grinned showing his white teeth. "We're almost there."

Chance nodded and followed the fox as he leapt down the stairs without caution. The stairs seemed to go on forever in long circles winding down, and down, and down. The air felt strange, like it was thickening, then thinning, and changing in weird ways, but the fox didn't seem to notice and just kept following the stairs down.

Finally they reached the bottom and the fox stopped at an archway that opened into a long dark hallway. "I can't go any further or he'll smell me coming."

CHAPTER SEVENTEEN

That's A Mighty Big Dog

Chance looked down at the fox. "Who will smell you coming?"

The fox stared down the tunnel into the darkness. "There's a dog that guards the book. He's big, mean and vicious, and he doesn't like it when anyone gets near it."

"So what am I supposed to do about this dog?" asked Chance.

"I have no idea."

Chance removed the crinkly yellow pages, and headed down the hall without another word.

The fox sat back on his haunches and watched her disappear into the darkness.

As Chance followed the dark hall, the walls gradually began to fade away. It was becoming lighter and the moldy, dusty smell in the air was being replaced by the scent of trees, flowers and fresh air. Now the hall had completely disappeared and was replaced by a path that led through a thick forest of splendid trees and a clear blue sky and she had the feeling that this place was very, very old.

Chance followed the narrow path through the trees, until she reached a small meadow that was covered in beautiful wildflowers of every imaginable color, shape and wonderful smells. In the center of the meadow, in the middle of all those flowers, was a small unadorned pedestal, and on that pedestal was a closed book.

Chance walked through the flowers and reached the pedestal and stared down at the book. This was too easy. She knew that something was wrong. It wasn't the book that bothered her; she knew it was the right book, because it was about the right size for the pages she held in her hand.

The book was the color of the sky, as it

looks from the top of a mountain, a dark, deep cobalt blue, other than that it was fairly plain, no fancy gold trim was around the edges or metal corners or special locks it just looked like a book, maybe a bit bigger than a normal book, but just a book. There was no title on the book, just a single golden symbol embossed right in the center. She rested her hand on the book and ran her finger around the edge of the symbol. She had no idea of what it meant or said, but she knew it was a magical marking that held power, not necessarily for good or bad, but a power to change things.

She was just about to open the book and fit the pages back in, when she spotted a linked golden chain that wrapped around the base of the pedestal. She followed the chain with her glance as it snaked through the flowers and up a low rise and down a shallow dip and disappeared into the trees at the edge of the glade. Seven had said there was a dog that guarded the book, and she knew she should hurry because it was probably just plain luck that he wasn't there, and it almost certainly wouldn't be long before he returned.

So she laid the crinkly yellow pages on the pedestal and tucked one end of them under unopened book so that the wind wouldn't blow them away and told herself that she wasn't a foolish girl for doing this as she followed the chain through the flowers and up the low rise and down the shallow dip and into the forest.

She followed the chain for a long ways, a lot longer than she thought she would have to, but eventually she came to the end, and saw a beautiful pond surrounded by cattails and lilies and duckweed and the biggest dog she had ever seen. The dog was curled in a ball at the edge of the pond, basking in the sun. He was black, deep, dark black with long fur and a long muzzle and long legs and blue eyes the color of the sea after a storm. His head was between two massive paws, and he was staring at Chance as she approached, but not in a scary way. She went right up to him, and sat down beside him and he hardly moved, and she started petting him behind the ears and down along his back; running her fingers through his silky smooth coat. He rolled over onto his side, and she scratched his chest and his foot started thumping and she knew he was happy to see her and she was happy to see him. She noticed that the long gold chain was attached to a collar that the dog wore around his neck. It also had a tag on it that looked just like the symbol on the book.

When he had enough he stood and stretched extending his front paws out and lifted his backside and yawned, showing off all his teeth and the spread of his jaws and his curled pink tongue. He sat back down on his haunches and Chance stood up so she could scratch his neck, but made the mistake of looking him in the eyes. That was a mistake. When she looked into them, she traveled up into the sky, and through the clouds, and out into the blackness of space, and past the planets, and beyond the galaxy right to the edge of the universe, and saw things that amazed her and frightened her and bewildered her. So she looked away and shut her eyes, and when she opened them again she wasn't sure where she would be, but happy when she saw that she was still standing next to the pond with the big dog.

The dog nuzzled her in the side and pushed her back a bit.

Chance pet him on the head. "Okay, okay, I know I don't belong here, but it's so quiet and nice and no one is trying to eat me, but I do want to get home and I know the fox does too."

Chance turned and followed the chain back through the trees and into the field of flowers and up to the podium where the book still sat and the crinkly yellow pages were still safely tucked under one edge.

Chance looked back, but the dog hadn't followed her, and she wondered why Seven was so scared of him. It must just be a fox thing. She lifted the edge of the book and picked up the crinkly yellow pages and flipped through them just to make sure the picture of the alley near her house was still there and she would have a place to return to. Chance realized then that there wasn't a portal in the forest, or at least anything that looked like a portal that would open up a doorway to her world, but then she remembered she wasn't looking through her shadow's eyes and maybe the portal was only visible in the shadow world. So she decided to take a quick peak and jump back if everything was still disorienting like it was in the hallway.

She shut her eyes tight and concentrated on her shadow's world and all the strange things in that world and when she opened them there wasn't a forest anymore. She was in a large square room made of stone and brick and mortar and totally the opposite of the forest she was in because this place was miserable and dark and frightening. There were long foreboding shadows on the walls and on the ceilings and she immediately felt trapped and imprisoned.

She was correct. The portal was only visible in the shadow world. It was big and round, maybe twelve feet in diameter, and located in the center of the room on a small platform. She could see herself through the portal standing in the forest right next to the podium with the unopened book still there, and it occurred to her that the book must be in her world and the portal in the shadow world.

Unfortunately she didn't have any time to think about this because she spotted the enormous black dog exploding from the forest and tearing through the field kicking up dirt and wildflowers in its wake. Its ears were laid flat against its head and there was fire in its previously beautiful eyes. It was charging directly at her, and it didn't look happy. Chance ducked, and she could see herself in the forest through the portal door, and she saw the dog leap over the podium and over her head and right into the shadow world. She was still looking through her shadow's eyes and spun on her heels as the dog flew over her head and tried to figure out what to do next.

She realized then that the dog didn't want her because when he hit the ground he never turned, he just kept going, and that's when she noticed there was only one way into and out of the room and she assumed that the hallway that lead to the forest was the same hallway that lead to this room in the shadow world. Chance then spotted Seven who must have just entered the room because she was sure he wasn't there a moment ago and he was yelling at her.

"Chance, open the book! Just open the book and...."

It all happened so fast she hardly got the

words out before the dog was already on him. *"Seven! Seven, get out of the way, get out of here...."*

Chance saw it all happen in slow motion. Seven had no chance and the massive dog pounced on him. But what happened next was something she never saw coming. Chance expected to see her friend lying there dying or already dead—but instead a thousand tiny birds made of mist and shadow and smoke burst out from under the dog where the fox had been a moment before and Chance realized that he really wasn't her friend after all.

CHAPTER EIGHTEEN

The Boy

The birds flew away from the dog and circled the room, melting into the shadows until they were one unbroken mass that swirled and spun around the ceiling with a life of their own. A section of shadow broke away from the mass and dropped to the floor in front of the girl, forming into something like a man with arms and a torso and a crown on its head—but where its legs should be there was darkness that snaked upward and joined with the shadows on the walls.

Then shadows all around the room began to take shape and form into terrifying creatures of all kinds each with a sword or spear or spike in its hands and they attacked the dog, driving him back in the direction of the portal. But the dog fought back and tore into the creatures tearing them to sheds vaporizing them with its claws and teeth and powerful blows from its massive legs. It doubled back and stationed itself in front of Chance protecting her from anything that came close, and vanquished everything in its reach. But in the end there were just too many of them and Chance could see that he was bleeding and badly hurt and couldn't fight much longer. She jumped in front of the dog and tried to protect him, but they ignored her and pushed her aside as though she didn't even exist. They doubled their efforts on the dog and were finally able to drive him back into the portal were he lay down and licked his wounds and watched them.

The Shadow King approached the girl. The dog started to get up and growled. She said to the Shadow King, "Why did you trick me like that? I thought you were my friend."

The Shadow King laughed a wicked laugh and she knew he was furious because he had come so close to escaping, and she had prevented that. "Foolish, foolish girl, all you have managed to do is trap yourself here as well. Soon enough, I will escape this place. Someone else will come along and free me."

Chance looked into the portal and to the dog and to the podium and to the pages that were still safely tucked under the edge of the book.

"I think I understand now. The book is in a place that isn't connected to shadow, and so you can't get to it. The portal is in this world, the shadow world, so you have the door to leave this prison, but you don't have the key to open it. You need someone from my world to open the book," said Chance. "The book is more than just a key back into my world. It's full of pictures just like the pages I brought back. It must be the way you can travel to all the places in the world throughout all of time. So if I would have put those pages back in the book, and opened it, I not only would have given you access to my world, but also to all of time," said Chance. "The irony here is that the book is still safe and unopened on the other side of the portal where you and your lackeys can't get to it, and now those final pages are with it and no one will stumble across them in my world and be able to find this place. …You will never be able to leave."

"Lock her in the dungeon," the Shadow King exploded to his guards, "and do with her as you please."

He exploded into mist and vapor, and she thought he must have rejoined the shadows that were swirling around the room. Then suddenly all of the light was sucked away and she was momentarily blinded, but as her eyes slowly adjusted she realized that he was in front of her and he put his nose up to her nose and she could feel the heat radiating from his eyes and the anger emanating from his ghost-like form. "Neither will you."

Then he was gone and his minions closed in.

She woke hours later in the dungeon.

"Hello, hello? Is anyone over there?"

Chance shook the sleep from her eyes and looked over at the wall where she thought she could hear a voice coming from. She was in a small filthy cell with slime and scum on the stone walls and ceiling and covering the floor. When she saw the door, tears welled up in her eyes because it was a wooden, solid door with no handle or lock or knob and she knew she was in the dungeon and now home seemed so far away.

Chance realized she had bruises all over her body, and her clothes were ragged and her backpack was gone and she thought it might now be okay to cry, but she wasn't ready quite yet. There was a small barred window no more than a foot tall and a few inches wide and the voice was coming through there. When she stood to look through the bars, she saw a boy's face. He saw her, and for a moment they smiled because now neither of them was alone and maybe, just maybe, there was hope.

"Hello, hello. Have they captured you as well?" asked the boy. "You aren't just another cruel trick are you?"

Chance was thinking the same thing, but when she looked into the boy's eyes she knew that was a real boy, and he was scared. He must have been three, maybe four years younger than her, and he was filthy and afraid, but holding back his tears. The boy wrapped his fingers around the bars, and Chance wrapped her fingers around his and smiled, and he smiled back and they both knew that they were in this together and neither one of them was a trick.

"How long have you been here?" asked Chance.

The boy looked at his clothes. "I don't know how long, it's so hard to say, I'm hungry and exhausted and they taunt me and I just want to go home. The monsters, the horrible ugly monsters have me trapped in here and I don't know what I've done."

Chance squeezed his fingers. "How did they find you and bring you to this place?"

The boy pulled back and thought for a moment. "My father needed work and he moved us to a town in Michigan. I tried to help them, and I sold candy and fruit to the passengers on the trains. One day a man walked by where I was selling candies and the strap on the satchel he was carrying broke and the contents of the bag spilled on the ground in front of me. There were papers and pencils and other kinds of objects and strange looking devices that I haven't seen before and I helped him collect them and put them back in his bag.

He thanked me and shook my hand, and I remember he looked kind of different than other people. His clothes looked like the kind of clothes a man would wear, but they just did not seem to fit right, and his face looked like a man's face, but there was something queer about it, and his eyes were a color that I had never seen before. And when he spoke, he spoke to me in English, but with a strange accent that I had never heard before. I assumed that he must have been a foreigner from some far-off land, but I didn't want to be rude, so I didn't ask. He packed up his bag and got on the train to Detroit, and just as the train started rolling away from the station I realized that we missed a few of the papers and I grabbed them and ran off after the train, but it had already pulled away."

Chance urged him to continue.

"I took the papers home with me that night and realized they must have been pages from a book, and old because they were crinkly and yellowed on the edges and stuck together where the binding should be," said the boy.

Chance was starting to get a weird feeling in her stomach, and she recalled the words that Miss Plink had told her... that sometimes seemingly insignificant events can add up to be something far more complex. "What was on those pages?" asked Chance.

"The pictures were like nothing I had ever seen before. There were four of them; one was a picture of a red barn surrounded by cornfields and some kind of contraption that looked like it was a machine with wheels, but I had no idea what it was. There was another picture of a dusty room with cobwebs in the corners and furniture all covered in blankets. The third picture was of an alley with bins over flowing with trash, but some of the trash didn't look right because it was in strange shapes and bright colors and fancy wrappers with words on them that I could read, but didn't make any sense. The strangest thing was that at the end of the alley I could see more of the wheeled machines and they had people in them and I could tell they were moving. The fourth picture I recognized. It was of the train station that I worked at and I knew exactly where the scene was, and I went there the following day and…."

Chance cut him off. "And you found a little doorway made from shadow and you walked through it and ended up here in this place."

The boy nodded. "Yes, that's exactly what happened! How did you know?"

Chance smiled. "Because I found the exact same pages and did the exact same thing, but instead of the train station I recognized that alley because that is right near where I live. But I can't figure out how I ended up with the same pages if you are here already! I would have thought they would be with the book, assuming that the Shadow King tricked you as well."

"Who's the Shadow King?" said the boy. "I never took the pages with me into this place. I didn't know where the doorway went, so I decided to leave the pages behind so the door would stay open. Didn't you think the same thing?"

Chance blushed. "No. I guess that never occurred to me. I brought them with me, and when I arrived I wandered around trying to get the doorway to reappear but I couldn't. So I found a path into the forest and found a fox," said Chance, who then filled him in on the rest of her story including everything she'd seen, and her ordeal to get here and the dog, and how the fox had tricked her, and how he was really the Shadow King, and she told him everything she knew about him."

"Wow, my story is hardly so exciting. I must have found the same path you had because I followed it for a short while into the woods so I might be able to figure out where I was, but I was attacked by some kind of huge wolf-like beast that dragged me back to this castle. The jailers searched me and tore the clothes from my body and forced me to answer all kinds of strange questions that I did not understand at the time, but now make more sense since you have told me your story. What bothered me the most was that all the time I was answering their questions I had the feeling that they already knew the answers, and knew me, and were somehow expecting me."

Chance thought about this for a moment. "Do you think the man that dropped those pages could have been the Shadow King?" asked Chance.

The boy shook his head. "No I don't think so. The man didn't seem bad or evil or anything like that, and you just told me the Shadow King is a prisoner here and can't leave this place."

"Yeah, I know, I don't get it either."

"Then who is he, and why do they think they know me?" asked the boy.

"I can't answer that. Maybe if you tell me who you are I might be able to figure it out."

The boy put one finger up to his lips. "Wait, I think they're coming in. Please don't leave. Just stay quiet," he whispered.

Chance nodded and slipped back down the wall into the shadows away from the opening of the barred window.

The troll threw the door open and stepped into the room, ducking to get through the door. He was horrible, nearly eight feet tall and wearing hardly any clothes. His skin was a dark shade of green and scaled like a lizard. His body was covered in scars, and wounds, and tattoos, and metal rings and chains. He walked over to the boy who was now huddling in the corner and effortlessly picked him up with an arm that was far too long for his body. Gently he ran a long, black, filthy fingernail down the boy's nose and the boy whimpered, but did not cry.

The troll turned him round and round studying him and poking him in the stomach, and pinching his arms and legs. "I thought I heard voices. Were you talking to your mum?" he asked with a harsh laugh.

For an instant the boy tried to squirm but the troll's hand tightened on him and he squeezed until Chance thought he would crush his ribs, but the boy never cried out he just stopped squirming and went limp. "Yes, I was talking to my mother. I want to see her. I miss her and just want to go home."

The troll laughed, shaking the boy and then tossed him in the corner. "Soon the Master will let us eat you; I just hope he does before you rot away."

The troll then appeared at the bars and looked directly at Chance and grinned.

The troll turned his back to the boy and hesitated at the doorway. He threw a metal plate of food into the room and watched it skip across the floor spilling and flinging brown slop off of it until it hit the wall and flipped over empty.

"Oops, it looks like you spilled your dinner. I guess it will just be water tonight," said the troll as he poured the contents of a pitcher onto the floor. "Oh how clumsy of me, I'll just go and fetch you some more."

Chance heard the door slam shut and the troll's laughter echo through the tunnel.

The boy appeared in the grate with an expression on his face that Chance will never forget. "Please…."

Chance started to shake, slid down the wall below the tiny bared window, and started to cry. She knew she needed to be strong for the boy, but for the moment she just wanted to be a little girl trapped in a dungeon in a place that no one would ever find her.

There was a skeleton with a shackle around its neck, attached to a chain that ran to the wall, and all she could think about was how long it might be before that was her. It was lying face down in the middle of the cell with one of its arms through a grate in the floor, and Chance thought that maybe she should have a look. So she fought back her tears and crawled over to the skeleton, peering through the bars to see what the poor creature had been trying to do, but it was too dark to see and she no longer had her flashlight or even the penlight.

Then she remembered the small flashlight, bigger than the penlight, but not nearly as big as the black aluminum one that was taken from her. She had placed it in her boot when the fox left her in the kitchen to clean herself up, at the time she didn't really have a reason to hide it there, it just seemed like a good idea, and now with it in her hands she was very glad she had.

She flicked it on, and hoped the a brilliant beam of light would slice through the bars like butter as it had so many other times in this place, but she also remembered Seven, the Shadow King, said it would only be just a flashlight while in the castle. Unfortunately when the beam came on it didn't slice through anything other than the darkness and she knew he wasn't lying about this. She angled the light through the grate and saw that the arm of the skeleton was reaching for a long rusted iron bar that presumably locked the grate shut. There was no padlock on it, but it was well out of reach of the bars and the only way to unlock it would be to turn the rod and push it out of the way, something that could only be done from the outside. But Chance saw an opportunity, and knew that she could use the skeleton's arm as an extension and maybe move the rod.

The boy had been watching everything. He saw her move over to the skeleton, and when he saw the beam of light illuminate from the flashlight his eyes sparkled and he couldn't wait any longer and called out to the girl in a whispered voice, "What is that thing?"

Chance waved her hand at the boy to quiet him down; the last thing she wanted was one of the jailers hearing them—this might be their only opportunity to get out. The boy clamped his hand over his mouth and watched in silence as the girl snapped the arm off the skeleton and pushed it out of the way. Then she took the tube with the glowing end on it and put it in her mouth so she could free up both hands and slid the skeleton's arm and both her arms through the grate as far as they would go.

With the flashlight in her mouth, it was difficult to see exactly what to do, but by twisting her head just right the beam lit up the locking rod and she could get a quick glimpse of its location. Then with all her might she jammed the skeleton's arm into it… and nothing happened. But she didn't give up, and she shoved the arm into the rusted rod over and over again trying everything to loosen it, and she kept doing it until she was exhausted and sweat dripped from her face. When she had about spent all of her energy and nearly gave up she tried one more time, and the rod did finally move. Slowly, very slowly she did this over and over again careful not to break or drop the arm and was eventually able to push it clear allowing the grate to fall open.

CHAPTER NINETEEN

Let's Get Out Of Here

The opening in the floor that the grate covered was barely large enough for her to squeeze through, but she managed to force herself though it, then grab a ladder that was connected to a narrow ledge about twenty feet below the floor of the dungeon. The ledge ran along the wall of a steeply sloped ramp that was directly below each of the dungeon cells. The ramp then traveled another fifty feet or so until it came to a hole that opened over the pit and she cringed when she realized what the purpose of the grate was for.

Chance followed the ledge to the ladder under the boy's cell and she climbed it until she could reach his grate. She let go of the ladder rung with one hand, and with the other stretched out until she could reach the locking rod.

Chance pushed on the rod until it slid out of the way and the grate dropped open. "Come on, we're getting out of here."

She helped him through the opening which wasn't that difficult because it looked like it had been days since he had last eaten. The boy started down the ladder then stopped and with his arm he reached back to the grate shutting it behind him. "Now maybe they'll think I was eaten. That should get them all stirred up trying to figure out who did it."

Chance dropped down to the ledge and climbed back up the ladder to her cell closing the grate behind her. "Good thinking… it might buy us a few extra minutes."

They found an opening in the wall that connected the ramp with the rest of the sewer system. When they had moved far enough away from the dungeon cells, Chance gave into exhaustion and sat down on the cleanest spot she could find.

The boy sat down next to her staring at the flashlight she had in her hand. "May I see it?"

Chance looked over at him. "See what?"

"That device in your hand that shines like a candle flame, but has no smoke and doesn't flicker or blow out when you walk," said the boy.

Chance just shrugged and handed it to him.

He twisted it around and examined it from every angle shining it in his face and at Chance and at the walls and the dirty sewer water and everywhere he could think of.

Chance heard the sound of squeaking and twisting, but before she was able to stop him the light suddenly went out and Chance grabbed for the boy. "Whoa, what did you do?"

Chance heard the same sound again and the light came back on. "Sorry about that, just trying to see how it works," said the boy as he tightened the battery compartment back down.

The boy handed the flashlight back to Chance and grinned. "What a marvelous invention."

Chance took the flashlight back and shined it on the boy to get a better look at him. "Who…?" but before he was able to speak they heard the sounds of many footsteps in the sewer behind them, and they doubted it was a coincidence.

"Time to go," whispered Chance.

The two of them raced down the tunnel as fast as they could, trying not to slip on the slime and filth that was everywhere.

"Where are we going?" the boy gasped out as he raced beside Chance.

"Not really sure, but I know we have to get back to the portal, and I know it's down here… somewhere."

The boy was getting tired and started to slow down. Chance realized that if she didn't find a way out quickly, this chase wasn't going to last much longer. It was time to get out of the sewer, and Chance stopped them at the next ladder they came to. At the top of the ladder was a small rectangular opening.

Chance dropped down the ladder and pushed the boy back up it. "I know where we are, just get up there and hide, I'll find another way out and come looking for you," said Chance as she forced him up the ladder and shoved him through the opening.

The boy grabbed her hands and tried pulling her through the opening. "They're right behind us; you'll never get away from them. I think you can make it."

Chance was shaking her head. "I can't fit, I'm too big."

"I think you might be mistaken," said the boy as he twisted her head in just the right way and yanked her out of the hole all the way up to her waist.

Chance pulled herself out the rest of the way and blushed. "I suppose I haven't eaten in a while. Come on, it's this way."

The two of them entered a long hallway, went down a flight of stone steps, and passed through a closed door, and stopped at the top of the narrow flight of stairs that led down into the darkness.

"Okay, we're almost there… this is a bit weird," said Chance.

The boy looked incredulous. "Weird? I think after all I've seen I can handle a little weird."

Chance grinned and led him down the stairs, and into the forest.

The boy's mouthed dropped open. "All right you win, I never saw this coming."

Chance stopped at the podium and looked down at the book, but didn't touch it. The dog stepped out of the forest and approached them; he was limping and looked exhausted, and

Chance felt horrible. He stopped next to them and Chance scratched him on the head. He nuzzled up to her nearly knocking her over just from his sheer size. The boy was fascinated by the dog and Chance was glad he wasn't afraid. There was something about the animal, even though he was huge and powerful and ferocious looking, she wasn't scared of him, and it seemed neither was the boy.

"It's time we end this… no more playing around," said Chance.

The dog seemed to understand what she meant and placed himself in front of the podium in about the same location where she thought the portal was in the shadow world. Chance pulled the pages out from under the book and flipped to the page of the train station, showing it to the boy. "This is your home, isn't it?"

The boy nodded.

Chance opened the book and she felt power well up from the pages and engulf her in a bath of energy that glowed with all the colors of the universe. The pages had vaporized when the book was opened, but she was pretty sure where they went. The boy's eyes grew wide when the pages disappeared, but she flipped to the end of the book and was very relieved when she saw her home and turned back a few pages and saw the boy's world.

She looked at him, and put her hand on his shoulder. "Are you ready?"

The boy looked up at her, with confusion in his eyes. "I suppose so."

Chance closed her eyes and started to think about the shadow world and everything she had seen there, but the boy stopped her and broke her concentration."

"You never told me your name," said the boy.

"You know I never did," said Chance. "It's Chance, Chance Nancy Counter."

The boy grinned from ear to ear. "Chance

N. Counter huh."

Chance just grinned. "Yup."

"My name is Tommy, Thomas Edison."

Chance did a double take, and all the pieces suddenly fell into place. "All of this, everything I've gone through, everything's that happened was all because I needed to find you...." She smiled and ruffled his hair with her hand. "I suppose this is what it's like to be part of a Rube Goldberg contraption," said Chance.

The boy just stared at her. "Excuse me?"

But Chance paid him no mind and she shut her eyes tight and concentrated again on her shadow's world and when she opened them she was there looking into the portal which no longer was a forest, but rather the train station just as it looked in the pages of the book. She grabbed the boy's shadow, pushed it toward the portal and shoved it into the opening and for an instant she saw the real boy as he was dragged behind by his shadow. For a moment the scene of the train station swirled and whirled and twisted around the boy as he moved through it expanding outward in glorious colors, and when he must have passed through, it solidified and she saw the boy standing there in his world waving back.

When Chance knew the boy was safe, she shut her eyes and made herself see through her own eyes again, which was always easier than seeing through her shadow's eyes. When she opened her eyes she was standing next to the podium in the forest with the book still opened to the train station. She started to flip the book to her page, but instead, closed the book altogether.

She walked over to the dog and scratched him on the back of the neck and rubbed his sides. "If I want to go home I'll have to open the book to the picture of my world, but if I do that it will leave the book open and the Shadow King will be able to escape."

The dog turned his head to her and whimpered.

Chance nodded. "You're stuck here too, aren't you? It's your job to guard the book, isn't it?"

The dog suddenly went rigid and growled a long, low, guttural growl that Chance could feel through his ribs.

Chance suddenly went stiff and she couldn't move her arms and she felt herself being dragged, but there was nothing around her. She knew that the trolls must have found her and captured her shadow, so she shut tight her eyes and forced herself to look through her shadow's eyes. When she opened them she was back in the shadow world surrounded by monsters with spears, and pikes, and swords and axes, and other implements of doom all pointed at the portal and at her. A troll had its arms wrapped around her shadow crushing and squeezing her, forcing the air from her body. She could smell his fetid breath and the stink of his body and it made her sick to her stomach and scared and angry because all she wanted to do was go home, and she was so close, and yet she knew she couldn't.

Then the Shadow King was there in front of her looking her in the eyes and laughing, but the troll was squeezing so hard that it was suffocating her and she was getting dizzy and started to drift in and out of consciousness.

The Shadow King swirled around her, whispering in her ears. "You can either open that portal for me now or I can send you back to the dungeon for a while, and because you seem so fond of escaping I think I'll have you chained to the wall this time. I believe a nice long stretch of quiet time in there might make you think twice about opening that portal for me. If not I can always put you on the dinner menu and let the trolls eat you… I'm sure they'd love that."

Then she blacked out.

She was out for only a second, because when she opened her eyes again she wasn't in the dungeon, she was on the floor in the portal room. Her arms were free and there was air in her lungs, but everything around her was in chaos, and she realized that the dog was the cause of it all. There were bodies all around her and she knew he must have leapt through the portal and attacked them to free her. She stood up and raced for the portal, but the Shadow King was there before she moved three steps. He twisted around her like a snake wrapping her in his shadowy coils tripping her and knocking her back to the ground.

"Where do you think you're going Chance?" whispered the Shadow King in her ear, but the girl only smiled back.

The Shadow King turned to see why she could possibly be smiling, but all he saw was the inside of the dog's gapping mouth an instant before being crushed between his teeth.

Chance was free again and she leaped to her feet on wobbly knees and headed for the portal which was still the scene of the forest with the book on the pedestal and her real body waiting for her, but when she tried to step over the threshold it went solid and she couldn't get through it.

Then the dog leapt through the barrier and slid to a stop in front of the real girl and hesitated for an instant until their eyes met. Through those eyes Chance once again saw the cosmos expand outward, and she was humbled again at how insignificant she was in the universe. Then she felt a great weight on her shoulders and realized that at that moment she was no longer just an insignificant spec and had just been given an enormous responsibility and that all of the inhabitants, of all of the planets, in that infinite expanse were now counting on her to take on a very significant burden. She dropped to her knees at the thought of what had just been asked of her and a tear ran down her cheek.

She took one long deep breath and got to

her feet, and finally lifted herself all the way up, taking the load onto her shoulders until she was standing straight and proud. She turned to the dog and looked him in the eye and nodded. The dog relaxed and his eyes turned blue, back to the color of the sea after a storm, and he smiled back in that way only a dog can. He walked over to the podium and gently picked up the book in his jaws and dropped it at Chance's feet.

She picked up the book and flipped to the end, the picture of the dirty smelly old alley that didn't go anywhere, with the dumpster and the overflowing trash cans and the stagnant puddles, and the shadowy doorway that did lead somewhere.

The dog lifted her off the ground and for a second everything went black and the world flip-flopped, but then she could feel the ground beneath her feet and she was standing next to the portal that was the scene of the alley and she wasn't sure if she was looking through her eyes or her shadow's eyes, but everything around her was total chaos. The shadows were bleeding from the walls, and from the floor, and from the ceiling, all flowing to the center of the room where they were fusing into a giant serpent-like creature made of mist and darkness and fury.

Where its eyes should be there were two infinitely black voids that absorbed the light from the room and radiated fear and hopelessness, and at that moment those empty voids were focused directly on Chance.

Chance could feel the weight of her responsibility pressing down on her and any resolve that she had found was leaching away and being drawn into the endless voids of the serpent's eyes. Her knees were buckling and she was losing hope, and faith, and the longer she stared the stronger the creature became and the more hopeless everything was becoming.

Chance fought the urge to give up, she fought and fought and fought far beyond the point of despair, but she didn't give up, and when she thought she had reached the breaking point she fought harder. Then she felt a spark ignite somewhere in the pit of her stomach, a spark she knew—she hoped—had always been there, and that spark grew and grew until it consumed her body and hope returned and all of the misery was washed away and she knew she had the strength to face the Shadow King and she wasn't afraid.

The Shadow King reeled back, his mental hold on the girl suddenly broke and with that his strength faded and he fell apart, scattering shadows to the four corners of the room.

Chance knew that she only had seconds before the Shadow King regained his strength and it was very unlikely he would lose again in a battle of wills—she could already see the shadows flowing back into the center of the room and begin reforming into the serpent. But before she could even think about her next move, the dog began pushing her into the portal. She could feel reality shifting, and the world melting away around her and everything was growing dark and her insides were twisting and swirling. She was still holding the book and it was open to her world and she wanted to go home, but she could see that the Shadow King had already reformed and was racing to the portal, trying to get at her or more likely trying to escape or for that matter probably both. But the dog stood between them and threw himself at the Shadow King and gave her the chance to make it through the portal and escape, but Chance couldn't let him do that.

Chance was pretty sure that once she was through the portal she could close the book and lock the Shadow King in that place, but if she did that she would also lock the dog in there with him, and with the portal closed and the book gone, he wouldn't be able to return to the forest where he was safe, and that was unacceptable. If she didn't do something, the Shadow King would kill him and she couldn't let that happen, she knew that her responsibility was to protect the book now, but regardless of that she had to help the dog.

Chance could feel her world pulling her home and she could hardly resist the urge to go back there, but she drew on her new found strength and forced her way back into the portal room and ran towards the dog and the Shadow King who were now in mortal combat. The Shadow King had the clear advantage. He was fresh and strong and powerful. The dog had been already been beaten and thrashed over and over again trying to protect Chance from the Shadow King and his minions, and he was weak and tired and hurt. The Shadow King had pinned him to the ground and the dog was struggling to get up, and Chance knew he couldn't take anymore. He had sacrificed his life to save her so she could protect the book, but Chance wasn't done yet.

"Hey, I'm over here. I'm the one you want not the dog," yelled Chance.

For an instant she had distracted the Shadow King and he turned his attention from the dog and eased his grip so he could see the girl… but that was his mistake and the dog took advantage of it. He pulled free of the Shadow King and struggled to his feet and with what energy he had left he leaped into the air and slammed into the Shadow King with all the force he could muster. The Shadow King was made of shadow and darkness and ancient energy, but the dog was made of stronger things and when he crashed into him it tore the energy that bound the Shadow King together, sending him into a thousand, thousand shadows.

The dog fell to the ground and skidded to a stop at the edge of the portal, exhausted. Chance looked to the center of the room and she could see the shadows coming together and reforming again so she grabbed the dog by his golden chain and pulled as hard as she could.

With all her will she pulled and pulled and pulled. "Come on, you're coming with me. You gave me this task to guard the book, and I will, but I don't want to do it alone. I can't do it alone, I need your help. And it's your turn, you've been trapped here long enough, I'm sure you're lonely and need someone who will let you live like a dog, and take you on walks, and rub your belly, and sneak snacks to you when no one is watching."

The dog looked up at her and she knew he understood and she could see him grin. He was the size of a bear, an immense bear, but Chance didn't care and she helped him stand on wobbly legs and led him by the chain into the portal. She felt the world flip flop, and she could feel her molecules tear apart into a billion pieces of energy and travel through the swirling darkness and incomprehensible gap that separated her world from the shadow world, then reform again just as she approached the edge of the barrier and the boundary to her world. When she emerged from the portal, to her relief, she still had the golden chain in her hand with the dog still attached and the open book in her other hand and she stepped over the threshold and brought them both into her world.

Once the dog was through, she turned to the portal and because the book was still open she could see through time and space and through the gap that separated the two worlds and into the portal room where the Shadow King had reformed. He saw her and their eyes met and he rushed to her gathering the darkness with him, covering the short distance across the room in an instant, but just as he was about to pass into the portal she slammed the book shut closing the door and trapping him in his world.

Chance breathed a sigh of relief, taking in the sights and smells of the dirty alley with its overflowing trash bins and murky, moldy puddles of water and fluorescent street lamp that glowed yellow in the fog. She was still looking at the wall, which was now just a wall again.

There were no shadowy doors or magic portals or strange symbols or anything else that made her think it was anything more than a wall, now it was just dirty old bricks like any other wall she had ever seen.

Chance had dropped the golden chain when she slammed the book shut and she noticed that the end of it was cut clean through and she assumed that when the portal slammed shut it must have severed the link and she realized that both she and the dog were truly free of that place. She picked up what remained of the golden chain and turned to the dog so she could remove it from his collar and it occurred to her now she was back in a normal place where having a dog that was the size of a bear might be a bit difficult to explain to her parents. And even if she did manage to explain it to her parents it might be a bit difficult to get them to let her keep him because it can't be very easy to take care of and walk and feed a dog that is the size of a bear.

When she had turned fully around to see that the dog was still there and hopefully figure out what she was going to do, to her astonishment, he had shrunk. He was the same dog with a black, deep, dark coat and long fur and a long muzzle and long legs and blue eyes the color of the sea after a storm, but he was no longer the size of a bear. He was more like the size of a dog, a particularly big dog, maybe about as big as a Great Dane or Newfoundland or Irish Wolfhound.

Chance placed the book under her arm, wrapped the chain around her palm, and they both walked out of the alley under the dim glow of the street lamp and into the fog and home.

EPILOGUE

Pearl Street station, lower Manhattan at 3 o'clock in the afternoon on 4 September 1882

Sweat drenched the technician saturating his clothes and smearing the soot that covered his face, but he had the fire hot enough to keep the water at a steady boil. The machines had started to function, the fire had generated enough heat to the boiler that it began to build a head of steam and transfer it to the motors and expand onto the face of the massive pistons forcing them to move in the cylinders. The connecting rods of the pistons strained, but it was enough force to turn the shafts and thus allow the huge rotors to spin in the jumbo dynamos. At the Pearl Street station in lower Manhattan, Edison's team installed six of these dynamos, each one weighing nearly 27 tons with an output of 100 kilowatts, enough to power the demonstration.

It was 3 o'clock and the time had come. The crowd had gathered and the news reporters were on site. There was no more waiting. It was time to display his work. Edison took a deep breath and pulled the switch allowing the current from the massive dynamos to flow. His team had wired 110 volts of DC current to 59 customers in lower Manhattan in the hopes of bringing electricity to the masses. The moment of truth was at hand and for a moment he thought it had failed, but then he started to see the filaments begin to heat and get brighter and brighter, and then all the bulbs began to glow, and he knew his vision had become reality. Everyone in the crowd cheered, and he grasped the fact that electricity could now be used to drive the darkness away, and only the rich would want to burn candles.

"Mr. Edison, Mr. Edison!" the reporters were all shouting his name.

Thomas Edison turned and chose a young man at the back of the crowd.

The rest of the crowd quieted and listened to what would be the first of a thousand questions.

"Mr. Edison, however did you come up with such an invention?"

Thomas Edison smiled. "I could not have done this alone. It was only because of the tireless hours of effort from everyone on my team through countless tests and hard work we were able to create this." He hesitated for just a moment and grinned a bit wider. "And I have to say some of it may just have been a bit by Chance."